Sweet So[1]

Millie Vigor

First published by Endeavour Press Ltd in 2017.

Table of Contents

Chapter 1

It was the first day of September, 1939, a time of harvest and gathering in, a time of endings and new beginnings. It was the day that Dorothea Jane Bartlett, Dorrie to those who knew her, was to say a final farewell to her mother. Summoned there by the tolling of a funeral bell she held her head high and looked neither left nor right as she entered the village.

Susan Jolliffe, purveyor of all things edible in the village shop, saw her passing by. 'That poor girl,' she murmured. 'What's to become of her now her mother's gone?' Already dressed in funereal black she picked up her hat and with a hat pin skewered it on her head. 'I'm going to the funeral, Jeannie,' she said to her assistant. 'Someone's got to show they care.'

'Right, then I'm coming too,' said Jeannie.

Susan and Jeannie fell into step behind Dorrie.

Jack Turner, Post Office, wools and haberdashery, turned the sign on his door to CLOSED and joined them. Geoff Smith, baker, left his son to watch the ovens and followed in the wake of Jack. By the time they reached St. Stephens, parish church of Monkton Priors, the little group following Dorrie numbered a dozen.

The church was cold and smelled of damp. A weak finger of late summer sunshine filtered through a window to point at a bunch of flowers on the coffin of Isobel Bartlett, mother of Dorrie.

The service was short. There were no hymns. Dorrie listened to the vicar and wondered how a man new to the village could sing the praise of a woman he didn't know. When it was over the little congregation followed the coffin to the graveside where they stood in respectful silence as the words of committal were uttered.

Susan Joliffe was to the side of and a little behind Dorrie. The girl, eighteen years old and now alone in the world, stood hands clasped and head bent while she struggled to contain her tears.

The coffin lowered, the symbolic handful of dirt thrown, the droning voice of the vicar uttered words of which Dorrie only registered "in sure and certain hope of the resurrection to eternal life," Condolences were offered. Dorrie accepted them and the firm clasp of hands with a watery smile and a thank you. As she turned away to leave Susan stepped forward and took her by the arm.

'You're coming home with me, Dorrie,' she said. 'I think you need a cup of tea and a bite to eat. I doubt if you've had anything yet, have you?'

Dorrie did not live in the village and other than Susan Jolliffe, there were no relatives that she knew of, or friends to invite to a wake for Isobel; there was to be no ham, no tea or shots of whisky, no people to surround her and help her over the first few hours of being alone. And Dorrie was grateful for the kindness of the woman by her side.

As they walked they came level with the war memorial in the centre of the village. Dorrie looked at it. It had been erected to commemorate the fallen of the Great War. The sounds of war were rumbling again in Europe and she wondered if it would affect Great Britain.

A young man holding the lead rein of a horse stopped and stood aside to let Dorrie and Susan pass by. Dorrie looked at him and felt a flush of colour diffuse her face as she looked at and loved his crop of dark hair and eyes of a deep dark blue that looked into hers.

So this was little Dorrie thought the lad. Her parents both dead there was now no one to keep her close. He smiled.

*

'Take your coat off and sit down while I put the kettle on,' said Susan when they were at last in her kitchen. 'What are you going to do now that you are on your own? You can't stay up there at Leanacres by yourself.'

'Why not?'

Susan busied herself with slicing bread and cutting cold beef to make a sandwich. 'It's not right, Dorrie, not right for a young girl to live on her own. It's not safe.'

Dorrie's home was the isolated cottage known as Leanacres, a cottage that had been built on the only few acres of productive land on the common a mile and a half from the village. When her father died Dorrie and her mother had struggled to keep it going and now that her mother was gone and she was alone the property was hers.

The child of elderly parents when she had arrived in the late summer of their lives she had been welcomed, nurtured and kept close. 'A blessing,' Isobel had said. All that Dorrie knew she had learned from them - care of

8

the house, the garden, the animals and all wild things. Leanacres was her home and she had no intention of leaving it.

'And where would I go, Mrs Jolliffe? I can't desert Leanacres, my mother and father worked hard to win a living out of it, poor it was at the best of times, but it's my home and I am not going to leave.'

There was no point in trying to persuade the girl otherwise thought Susan, so she fed her, sympathised, then sent her on her way, but not before telling her that if ever she needed a shoulder to cry on she was to come to her. Then she waved her off and watched as she walked away.

Half a mile from the village Dorrie turned off the tarred road, opened a gate on to the common, then walked the mile long track to the cottage. Built of stone it crouched low and turned its back to the wind. To the west of it was a barn, some small buildings, a garden, and a couple of paddocks. A cow grazed in one. There was no flower garden to the front of the house, just an area of bare earth where chickens scratched. A solitary climbing rose struggled to survive on the wall beside the door. Dorrie patted the head of the dog that rose to greet her then opened the door and walked in.

*

She was stringing beans when Susan Jolliffe knocked on and opened her door a few days later. 'Hello, Dorrie. Are you there?' she called as she walked in. 'It's such a nice day I thought I'd come to see you. I didn't realise you were quite so far from the village though. It's a long walk.'

'I suppose it is a bit out of the way,' said Dorrie.

'You can say that again.' Susan Jolliffe pulled a chair out from the table and sat down. 'Are you lonely now you're on your own, or do your friends come to see you?'

Dorrie allowed herself the suspicion of a smile. 'Nobody comes, Mrs Jolliffe. I don't really know anyone, you see.'

'My goodness, why did your parents keep you so isolated? It's a good job I decided to come today because I have the cure for that,' said Susan. 'I came because Jeannie has left me and I want someone to give me a hand in the shop. Would you come and work for me?'

A smile crept across Dorrie's face. A job was just what she needed. 'Yes, I'd love to,' she said. 'What would you want me to do?'

'You don't have to be a genius. It's nothing more than weighing up stuff and serving the customers. Someone to help gives me time to write up the books and such. I think you're just the person I'm looking for. As well as a wage I can give you a dinner every day. How does that sound?'

Dorrie smiled. Better and better! A job close to home and dinner, too.

While she waited for Dorrie's reply Susan drummed her fingers on the table. 'Well, that's it,' she said at last. 'I've decided. You'll be at the shop at ten o'clock tomorrow. Don't be late.'

'I haven't said yes.'

'But you were going to. I need you and you need me. I'll be expecting you tomorrow. There'll be an apron to cover your clothes.' Susan Jolliffe got to her feet and pushed her chair back under the table. 'I see you've got quite a bit of garden. How are you going to keep it up on your own?'

'I've always done the gardening,' said Dorrie as she followed Susan out of the house. 'Come and have a look at it.'

'But you're growing far too much,' said Susan when she looked at the rows of potatoes, beans and cabbage. 'What are you going to do with it all?'

'When Dad was alive he used to take some of it to town to sell,' said Dorrie. 'I shall have to do the same but I have to find a way to get it there.'

'Hm. I'll take some. Your stuff will be fresher than what I get. I'll let you know how much I want and when. What a good thing it was I decided to come. I'll see you tomorrow.'

Good things happened as well as bad thought Dorrie. A job and a pay packet would give her money for her pocket and an outlet for her produce. The worry of how she was going to pay the bills that kept coming in had been lifted.

'We're going to be all right, Moss,' she said as she ruffled the dog's head. 'I'll get you a bone from the butcher tomorrow.'

Chapter 2

Dorrie presented herself at Susan's door promptly at ten o'clock. She donned the apron that was handed to her then watched and listened as she was shown what to do. She was quick to learn and it didn't take her long to settle in or to get to know the customers. She listened to their grumbles, their worries about the war and their hopes that it would soon be over. She laughed with the younger ones when they told her what their children said and did.

Susan watched her as she worked. Dorrie was not like the village girls who giggled and flirted and forgot what they were told within a matter of minutes. There was an air of serenity about her. She walked with grace. If something should spill or get overturned she never became flustered or irate, as Jeannie often had, but calmly put things to rights.

'I'm so glad you decided to work for me, Dorrie,' said Susan.

'I rather think it was you who decided,' said Dorrie.

'Well, maybe it was.' Susan laughed. 'You know, don't you, that Britain is now at war with Germany?'

'Is it? When did that happen?'

'It was on the news, yesterday. Neville Chamberlain said that we were at war. You do know, don't you, that Hitler's rampaging over Europe?'

'Yes, I knew that, but not the other.'

'Well, mark my words. It will go down in history that on the third day of September our prime minister announced on the radio for all to hear that Britain was now at war. Don't you have a radio?''

'No, I don't, but we sometimes used to get a newspaper.'

Susan stopped what she was doing and turned to look at Dorrie. 'Why did your dad keep you all shut away up at Leanacres? He wasn't a criminal, was he?'

Dorrie laughed. 'No of course he wasn't, but there wasn't the money to spare for things like radio's and when he went to other places to work he would get all the news that mattered from other people. I don't think it did me any harm.'

Maybe, and maybe not, thought Susan. 'Have to see if I can get hold of one for you. It would be company for you in the long evenings.

And there the matter was left.

*

'There's something about that girl that I can't put my finger on Reg,' Susan said to her husband as they sat down to their tea. 'It's hard to believe that Reuben was her father. She looks as though she should be dressed in silks and satin and not that faded old cotton dress that I swear she washes and dries overnight ready to wear next day.'

'She must get it from her mother,' said Reg Jolliffe. 'Nobody knew where she was from and I always thought she was too good for Reuben.'

'You might be right. Isobel was well spoken and she wasn't like folk round here, a bit better class you might say. Perhaps she and Reuben had to get married and didn't want anyone to know and that's why they chose to live where they did.'

'That can't be right. Dorrie wasn't born 'til they were near past it.'

'No, she wasn't, was she? Oh well it ain't none of our business.'

*

It was late in the day when Garnet Plowman walked into the shop. A handsome, dark haired lad, twenty years of age, broad shouldered and muscular, he seemed to fill the space between the sacks of potatoes and swedes and the counter behind which Dorrie stood.

'What can I get you?' she asked.

'I'll have you for a start,' said Garnet. He laughed and took a step closer.

Dorrie blushed and hung her head. 'I'm not for sale,' she said.

Garnet put his hands on the counter and leaned towards her, 'So what do I have to do to win you?'

'I'm not a competition prize either.'

'Now then Garnet, behave yourself,' said Susan as she came through from her living quarters. 'Dorrie deserves a good man so you have to be a gentleman.'

Garnet turned a winning smile on Susan. 'Ah, Mrs Jolliffe, now you know I can be that.'

'So you might and so you mightn't, but what did you come in for?'

Garnet was shopping for his mother. He took a piece of paper from his pocket and gave it to Susan. While he waited for her to put together the things he required his gaze never left Dorrie. She was shy and wouldn't look at him and he realised that because her parents had kept her tucked away she had never been in the company of a young man before and didn't know how to handle the situation. She was not like the cheeky village girls he usually consorted with. If he wanted to get to know her he was going to have to tread softly.

'Here you are then,' said Susan as she handed Garnet a bag of goods. 'Are you going to pay me now?'

'No, mother will next time she comes in.'

'Off with you then.'

Susan Jolliffe licked the end of her pencil and wrote the sum of ten shillings and six pence in a notebook. She closed it up and put it in a drawer under the counter. Then she looked at Dorrie and saw that the girl was watching the retreating back of Garnet.

'He's a nice lad,' she said.

'He's nothing to me,' said Dorrie, too quickly.

'Better let it stay that way then. Just sweep the floor and tidy up ready for tomorrow then you can hang up your pinny and put your coat on. I'm sure you've got things to do at home and I can see to anyone else who comes in.'

*

With the evening stretching before her Dorrie didn't hurry home. It didn't matter if it was dark before she milked the cow. She had a lantern to provide light, not that she needed it, for who but an idiot would not be able to milk a cow in the dark? On her old bicycle she pedalled along and got off to push it up the hilly bits, where if she was in a hurry she would ride. When she reached the common she got off her bicycle, opened the gate, pushed it wide, then stopped.

'Well, here you are at last.' Garnet Plowman was sitting on the bank.

'What are you doing here?'

'I wanted to see you again.'

'Well, you can't.'

'I don't see why not, you look pretty solid to me.'

Garnet stood and took the bike from Dorrie. He wheeled it through the gateway. She stood with her hand on the gate. 'I'm not going to shut it until you're on the other side of it,' she said.

'Why, what are you afraid of?'

'Nothing, but I have work to do. I can't stay here talking to you.'

His face broke into a grin and it was Dorrie's undoing. Oh, but he was handsome! What beautiful children he would have. The thought of it made Dorrie's heart beat a little faster.

'Ah, won't you let me walk a little way with you?' pleaded Garnet.

Dorrie paused, then her voice curt she said, 'Well . . . a little way . . . if you like. But not far.'

She kept her bicycle between them and concentrated on pushing it. For a while neither spoke then Garnet said, 'Are you lonely, Dorrie, now your mum's gone? I saw you going home from the funeral.'

'That was you with the horse, wasn't it?'

'Yes.' They walked on in silence.

Dorrie stopped. 'You can't come any farther. Go home.'

'But . . .'

'Go home, I said.'

'No, I'm not going to. I'd like to see you again. I'd like to take you out somewhere, please say I can.'

'Why would you want . . . '

'Look, just say yes and then if you decide that you really don't like me, well that's it, isn't it?'

'I don't know. I mean . . . where would we go? What would we do?'

'I could take you to the pictures or we could have a picnic. The weather's just right for that.'

Time stretched between them before Dorrie replied, 'All right, but just the once, eh?' Without waiting for an answer she hopped on her bicycle and rode away.

Garnet watched her go. One day he would win her for himself. He would take her in his arms and kiss her 'til she begged him to stop. But he wouldn't. He would lay her down, explore her body and rouse the passion that he knew was sleeping in her and he'd carry on until she could refuse him no more. She would be his.

Chapter 3

Susan put cups of cocoa on the counter. 'They're going to put butter and bacon on ration next month,' she said.

'Are they? I wonder what it will be next. I think I ought to sell the cow, Susan. I don't need all that milk. Can I put a notice in the window?'

'Of course you can.'

On a piece of paper Dorrie wrote, COW FOR SALE. SHE IS A GOOD MOTHER AND GIVES PLENTY OF MILK. SHE IS EIGHT YEARS OLD AND HER NAME IS BLOSSOM. BEST OFFER SECURES.

As she fastened it to the window with a piece of sticky tape a horse and cart came to a halt outside. Garnet hopped down from his seat on the shafts, opened the shop door and looked in. 'I can't stay now,' he said. 'Just thought I'd stop and tell you to meet me by the cenotaph at three o'clock on Sunday. We'll go for that picnic. You don't need to bring anything.'

'But I can. Where will we go?'

'Ah, that'll be my surprise. I've got to get on.' Wiggling his fingers at her he closed the door. Dorrie watched as he swung himself up on to the shafts of the cart, snapped the driving rein on the horse to get it moving, and drove away.

'He's a nice boy,' said Susan as she stood beside Dorrie to watch the cart trundle down the street. 'You could do a lot worse.'

*

When Sunday came, anxious not to be late for her date with Garnet, Dorrie put hard boiled eggs, lettuce and tomatoes along with a bottle of cold tea in a bag, hung the bag on the handle bar of her bicycle and was ready.

'I'm sorry, Moss,' she said as fondled the dogs head. 'But I've got to go. Look after the house and I'll see you later.'

She was at the cenotaph at three on the dot, but Garnet was already there. 'You're early,' she said.

'That's because I couldn't wait to see you. Come on, follow me.'

It was just a short ride to the place Garnet had chosen for the picnic and pedalling along through the narrow lanes behind him, Dorrie exulted in a freedom that had been so long coming to her.

It was a mellow October day, the last gesture of a dying season. When they reached the picnic spot Dorrie was entranced and gazed in wonder at a water mill, the mill race and the green sward beside it.

'I never knew this was here,' she said.

'I thought you might not,' said Garnet, 'that's why I brought you.'

Water chuckled happily as it bypassed the now silent wheel and flowed on to join the wide expanse of the mill pond beyond. The surface of the pond was still. It reflected the blue of the sky and little clouds that floated lazily across it. From the reeds that bordered the pond came the harsh kurruk call of the moor hen. The trees of the wood behind the mill house flaunted their autumn colours, the gold of the beech trees contrasting sharply with the lingering green of oaks. From somewhere among their branches pigeons cooed softly.

'Put your bike down,' said Garnet. 'I've got something to sit on.'

'It's too soon to eat,' said Dorrie as she sat down on a rug Garnet had spread for her. 'But I brought some eggs and salad.'

'You didn't need to do that. Mum made some sandwiches for us and I brought a bottle of pop. But now I've got you to myself, talk to me. I want to know everything about you, Dorrie. I want to know what you like, what you don't like, and what you plan to do with the rest of your days.'

'That's a tall order, Mr Plowman,' Dorrie laughed. 'It'll take a long time so how long have you got?'

Garnet put his arm round her shoulders and pulled her close. With his lips in her hair he said, 'The rest of my life, how about you?'

The pounding of her heart chased Dorrie's laughter away. She could feel the warmth of his body and the hardness of the strong arms that held her. This was too soon. 'You might not like what I tell you,' she said.

'Tell me anyway. Tell me why your mum and dad kept you close and only rarely let you come to the village? Tell me why I never got a chance to see you before.'

Garnet's head was next to hers, his cheek against her cheek. If she turned towards him he would kiss her.

'I had to work. There was always such a lot to do. My mother was not well so I had to look after her and do the work she would have done. I was not a prisoner although it may have seemed that way.'

'And now she's gone as well as your father. Aren't you lonely?'

'No, I'm not. I've got my job in the shop and when I'm home I work in the garden. I've got my dog and she's the best company ever.'

Garnet turned Dorrie to face him. 'And now you've got me. I love you, Dorrie Bartlett.' He smiled as he bent his head and covered her mouth with his. She closed her eyes and melted. When he let her go she sighed. He smiled and hugged her to him.

'Look, look there,' he pointed at a bird on the pond. 'That's a moor hen, that's the one you heard just now.'

Dorrie watched the moorhen paddle away and disappear among the reeds that grew at the edge of the pond.

'It's a lovely little bird, isn't it? Did you know,' said Garnet, 'that for its size the moorhen is very aggressive. It's vicious. It often fights other males and can cause injuries. You wouldn't think birds would do that, would you? And then there are the coots. They're bigger than the moorhen, but they're as bad if not worse. They go out looking for trouble.'

'No, I didn't know that,' said Dorrie.

Garnet chuckled, threw himself back on the ground and lay there laughing. 'And why would you want to.'

His laughter was infectious. Despite herself Dorrie began to laugh too. 'You're teasing me,' she cried.

'Yes, I am. But it's true. As they say, nature is red in tooth and claw. Sorry, but now you're laughing too and I love to hear you laugh. Did you say you'd got eggs and salad? Are the eggs hard boiled?'

'Yes, they are, and if you don't behave yourself I shall throw them at you.'

'Oh don't do that, come here and let me kiss you to say sorry.'

They stayed by the mill and ate their picnic. Dorrie talked, Garnet flirted, and they laughed and got to know one another. They stayed until the afternoon drew to a close; stayed until the cooing of the pigeons in the trees sang a soft lullaby and the dusk of evening wrapped itself round them.

'I must take you home,' said Garnet as he pulled Dorrie to her feet. As she stood he took her into his arms.

'It's nice here. I'd like to stay,' she said. 'I'd like to have a house and live in a place like this. I like the trees and the birds and the sound of water.'

'I'll build you one someday,' said Garnet. 'Not here but somewhere, one with trees and birds and animals and just you and me. Would you like that?'

'I'd love that. But all that's a long way off.'

'I know, but you've got to have dreams, Dorrie, dreams that if you work hard at might someday come true.'

Dorrie smiled. 'I love your dreams, Garnet; but I've got to go home. I've got a cow to milk.'

Garnet dropped a kiss on her forehead. 'Talk about bringing me back down to earth. You're right though, I've kept you out long enough. Let's go.'

Chapter 4

With a rope on the cow's halter, Dorrie led Blossom to the village and tied her to the trunk of a small tree growing in the hedge beside the shop. There she would stay until Farmer Pascoe, the man who had travelled up to Leanacres to inspect the animal, came to collect her. Dorrie stroked the satin of the cow's cheek, sighed to think that one more link to her old life was being broken before telling herself she 'had to get on with it,' and went into the shop to begin her work.

It was midday before the farmer arrived to collect Blossom. He came in a pony and trap, paid Dorrie in cash, tied Blossom to the back of the trap, hopped up, clicked his tongue at the horse and drove off. Susan came to stand beside Dorrie as she watched them go.

'Everything changes, doesn't it?' said Susan. 'We get bogged down in our little lives and hope that's the way it will stay, but it doesn't. So we have to get on with it whether we like it or not.'

'That would be it, Mrs Jolliffe.'

'And we've got a shop to run so we'd better get on with that, too.'

Customers came and went, there were busy times and slack times, and the day went on much as usual. When at last the shop was closed and Dorrie put on her coat and hat ready to go home she wondered if Garnet would be waiting for her beside the common gate. He often was and she looked for him and felt her heart leap when she saw his smiling face. When he wasn't there the sun dropped out of the sky and she walked under a cloud. Life would be so dark and dreary without him. But then he would be there again and a rainbow would arc across the sky.

In her heart she nursed the memory of their day beside the mill and often smiled secretly as she thought of how he made her laugh. Laughter had been absent from her life for a long time. It was good to be able to share it with someone again. He had declared his love for her and she was sure that the feeling his presence stirred in her was love, too. She wanted his kisses, wanted his arms around her, wanted him to be part of her life and wanted him to be there at the gate waiting for her.

But he was not because when she stepped out he was leaning against the wall of the shop. When she asked him what he was doing there he told her he had come to escort her home because he didn't want anyone to rob her of the vast amount of money she had been paid for her cow.

'Oh don't be silly,' she had said. 'I would have been quite safe.'

'So I'll go home then, shall I?'

The smile that had warmed her face when she saw him suddenly faded. "He means nothing to me," she had said to Susan Jolliffe. That was no longer true. He was everything to her. He was the one thing that made the routine of every day worthwhile. He was the one who made the moon shine, who put the sparkle in the stars. What would she do if he walked away and left her on her own? Tears pricked her eyes. She blinked them away.

'Please don't go,' she said.

He laughed. Came to her and lifted her chin with his finger. 'Ah no, you're upset,' he said. 'Don't cry. I was only teasing.' Gently he put his hand on her arm, turned her and with her by his side, started to walk.

Step for step Dorrie walked beside Garnet. Though he usually chattered away when they were together he was not talking now. I wonder what's going on in his mind she thought. When they reached the common gate Moss was there to greet them.

'Does she always come to meet you?' asked Garnet.

'Yes, and it doesn't matter what time it is she's there. She likes you. You're honoured because she doesn't like everybody.'

'So she's not going to bite me if I kiss you then,' said Garnet as he pulled her into his arms.

'No, of course not,' said Dorrie. She nestled close to him and lifted up her face for him to kiss. Never before had she been held like this. Never before had she felt so safe or as protected as she was in the circle of his arms. Never before had she felt so loved.

Holding her close Garnet buried his face in the softness of her hair. He held her close, could feel the warmth of her, and with his hands inside her coat, the curve of her back. He had planned to win her and persuade her into letting him make love to her and would have overruled any protestations she might have. But now that he knew her better it seemed such a callous thought. What he should have been thinking of was how he would fill her days with sunshine and make her feel happy and secure.

He hadn't bargained for, hadn't realized just how much she was going to mean to him, how much he was going to love her or how she might feel about him. Winning her was not a game.

"Please don't go," she had whispered when he had jokingly said he should go home and he knew she had been thinking of her mother. So how was he going to tell her that he had to leave her too? Had to go and fight for his country. He would come back though, oh yes, he would come back. That is if he wasn't blown up by a mine or if he didn't meet a German bullet head on.

'Dorrie,' he said. 'I love you and I never want to leave you or hurt you.'

'Then don't.'

He tightened his arms around her. 'But sometimes things happen that we can't control, can't do anything about, so maybe I won't be able to help it.' He nuzzled her neck. She smelled warm and womanly and with a hint of the soap she washed with. 'There's something I have to tell you. I don't know how . . . oh, damn, I can't.' He pushed her from him, walked away then looked back. She stood where he had left her.

'Dorrie. Dorrie. Oh God.'

Her face puckered into a sad smile. 'You don't have to tell me,' she said. 'You're going to go away and leave me, aren't you?'

'How do you know, who told you?'

'Nobody, but it's what happens. Everybody leaves me, my father, my mother and now you.'

He ran back to her. 'I don't have any choice. I've been called up. There's nothing I can do about it; like everybody else I have to go. But I will come back. Wait for me, Dorrie. Say that you'll wait for me? Say you will, say it.'

'Of course I will,' she said. 'How could you doubt me? Of course I'll wait.'

She was going to be alone again. Why was life being so unkind? Her mother could not come back and neither would her father. And now Garnet was going to leave her too. When she was on her way home from work he would not be there by the gate to look at her and warm her heart with his smile. He would not be there to thrill her with soft kisses on the back of her neck, would not be there to hold her. And she would have to walk without the feel of his strong arm round her waist.

A line from Shakespeare's *Romeo and Juliet* flooded into her mind. *"Parting is such sweet sorrow that I shall say goodnight till it be morrow."*

How many morrows would it be 'til Garnet was there again?

'How soon, how soon do you have to go?' she asked.

'Tomorrow, I leave tomorrow. I couldn't tell you before. Oh Dorrie.' He seized her in his arms and crushed her to him so tight that she was afraid her ribs would crack. 'It breaks my heart,' he sobbed. 'Promise me you'll wait for me. Give me that to hang on to.'

'I promise.'

There was not much time left. Not much to make the most of what she had. Not much in which to make and store a memory that she could recall when her days were long and empty. She knew that she loved him, loved him more than she had ever dreamed. She wound her arms round his neck and melded her body to his. He kissed her, gently at first, then with rising passion. The feelings that coursed through Dorrie were ones she did not want to quell.

As they stood there, neither wanting to part, day crept past them and turned to night. Above them, the moon, with no care or worry about what was happening on earth, sailed serenely on.

'I must take you home,' said Garnet. Again, step for step, she and Garnet walked side by side.

'Don't go,' she said. 'Please don't go.'

'Darling Dorrie, there's nothing I can do about it. I have to.'

'But not yet, and I mean now. You can't go 'til I let you so sit down and talk to me, tell me about when you were a child, about school and what you wanted to do with your life so that I have something to remember.'

'I thought I already had.'

Dorrie sat down on the sun-baked turf of the common. She patted the ground beside her and Garnet joined her. 'Not half enough,' she said. 'I want to know all about you. When you're away will you write and let me know how you are?'

'I'm not very good at writing.' Garnet, his arm round her shoulders, nuzzled her ear. 'Do you love me, Dorrie? You've never said.'

'Do I love you?' she smiled. 'What a silly question. *"Let me count the ways, I love thee to the height and depth and breadth my soul can reach.*" Of course I do. I love you Garnet Plowman and don't you ever forget it.'

'And when I come home will you marry me, Dorrie Bartlett?'

'Yes, oh yes,' she said, and putting her arms round his neck she pulled him down to lie beside her. His kisses were passionate. She kissed him back with equal passion. The warmth of him and his nearness excited her. When he brushed his hand softly over her breast desire coursed through her body.

'Don't stop,' she said when he held back to look at her.

'But . . .'

'Shhh, the man in the moon is watching us.'

'He should mind his own business,' said Garnet.

A cloud drifted across the sky, obliterating the face of the moon, and the man up there saw nothing more.

Chapter 5

Gradually, the young men of the village who laughed to cover their fear of what might be, who promised to write every day and who said that it would be no time at all before the war was over and they would be back, left their homes and went away. The baker's son, a serious young man who looked as though he should be sitting behind a desk and not kneading bread, was there one day and gone the next. When he came home on leave, clad in a rough khaki uniform, a jaunty forage cap on his head and his feet in tough black boots, he was unrecognisable. Susan Jolliffe's son kissed his wife, hugged his children and said goodbye to his mother and cursing his luck, boarded a bus and was carried off. Some volunteered and some were conscripted, but they all left the village by whatever means until only the old men, the infirm, or those in essential occupations were left.

So much had changed for Dorrie since her mother had died. She had dreamed of leaving home, it would have been an adventure; she would have been able to do so many of the things she had only read about. But now she had the responsibility of the house and land and unless she sold it she was tied to it. She had met Garnet, fallen in love with him and thought she'd found the end of the rainbow. But even that precious pot of gold was to be denied her and, but for a few precious hours when he'd come home on embarkation leave, he had been taken from her too. Save for one scribbled note on a scrap of paper to tell her he was in France and that he was all right there had been no more. He was gone and she knew not where.

Perhaps all things conspired to persuade her that it was time for her too to spread her wings and fly. Perhaps it was time to seek new horizons. Perhaps she had to accept that it was time to lock up the house and join one of the services too. On her next trip into the town she would find the enlistment office and sign on.

*

'They say the war won't last long but I don't believe them,' said Susan Jolliffe. 'They said that last time and look what happened. Thousands of men killed, thousands of women made widows and children fatherless and for why? Well I'll tell you, it's because them that go to war send their men to fight their battles for them. Years ago kings and princes used to fight alongside their soldiers. You won't catch them doing that now.' Susan shook her head and sighed. 'So many young men have to lose their lives, it's not right. Death comes to all of us,' she said. 'We can accept it when it comes to those who have lived a full life, but it's very hard when we have to lose our young men. I feel for the ones on the ships that are bringing us food. The Germans are trying to sink them and starve us into submission.'

'I think they'll have a job to do that,' said Dorrie.

'But I don't know if we can grow enough to feed us all, we need to import the stuff that we can't. It seems that something else is going to be rationed every day. Sugar is next on the list. How are we going to make jam? And meat will be rationed as well and I'll guarantee it won't end there.'

'We've got vegetables, Mrs Jolliffe. And there's honey and plenty of rabbits so we needn't go short of meat.'

Dorrie was adept at making a penny do the work of two. She had learned from her mother how to make the carcase of a chicken provide meals for several days. She had learned how to set a snare and catch rabbits, how to roast them or make a stew. She also knew the trick of catching a pheasant, but if you asked her how she wouldn't tell you. When it came to vegetables her father had taught her how to grow enough to last throughout the year. So though there may have been a shortage of money in the Bartlett household there was never a shortage of food and the thought of it being rationed did not unduly upset her.

When she wondered how she would manage after her mother had died she thought about her father. Faced with any problem his answer was always the same, "We go on as before." She often repeated it to herself, always adding that it was not true. The loss of her mother and now Garnet changed everything. But though there was no news of Garnet he would come home. And then the thought assailed her that he would if he was lucky. She'd had a letter from him, a note scribbled on a sheet of paper signed with love followed by a row of kisses just to let her know he was all right. But there had been nothing since. Dorrie sighed and Moss, picking up on her mood, laid her head on Dorrie's knee.

'It's all right Moss; it's just me being a bit sentimental, just wishing that this war wasn't happening and that Garnet was here with me. But I have you don't I, so I'm not alone.' She patted the dog's head then got up and put her letter away in a safe place.

*

Signing on had been easy, but now, divested of her clothes, Dorrie was waiting to be examined by a doctor to find out if she was fit enough for the rigours of an active life in the army, the ATS. She was apprehensive and wished there was someone with her if only to mentally hold her hand.

'Now young lady,' said the doctor when it was Dorrie's turn to be examined, 'you look as though you've spent most of your life out of doors. Would I be right?'

'Yes, that's right,' said Dorrie.

'Thought so, you look healthy.'

When heart, blood pressure and lungs had all been tested and Dorrie had answered innumerable questions about her health in general she sat on a chair and waited while the doctor filled in a form. Hands clasped tightly together she was anxious to hear if she had passed.

'One more question,' said the doctor. 'Are your periods regular, no troubles in that department?

'Um . . . well . . .'

'Why do you hesitate?' The lady doctor looked at her. 'I guess they're not. Get up on the bed.'

Dorrie climbed on to the examination bench and lay there while the doctor pressed and prodded her stomach then shook her head and tut-tutted. 'Okay,' she said. 'You can get down now, but you can forget about the army, you're pregnant.

Dorrie slid off the bench and stared at the doctor.

'What?'

'My dear girl, where have you been? You're going to have a baby. Get your clothes on and go home and next time make sure your boyfriend uses some protection.'

*

Winter brought snow so Dorrie left her bicycle at home and trudged to work in a pair of wellington boots that Susan had given her for Christmas. Susan had invited her to join her family for the day. Dorrie said she would be delighted but only if she could provide a chicken for their dinner. In fact one chicken was not enough for Susan and her husband, who were joined by their son's wife and three grandchildren. Dorrie was drawn in and treated as one of them and so different was the day to the sober Christmas's at Leanacres that Dorrie could not disguise the tears of happiness that welled in her eyes. 'Come, come,' said Susan, 'no tears today. Pull the wishbone with me.' Dorrie did and the lucky piece was hers. She smiled and wondered how long she would be able to keep her secret.

One day when the sun sent shafts of golden light through her windows, when spring crept over the horizon and the days began to lengthen, did Dorrie decide it was time for spring cleaning. She opened the door to her mother's bedroom and walked in. Taught to respect the privacy of others, it was the first time she had done so since Isobel had gone.

An iron bed, one of the brass knobs of the bed posts missing, its sagging middle piled with blankets on which an overcoat had been thrown, took up most of the room. An alarm clock as dead as the people who once occupied the bed stood on a chair beside it. A wooden blanket box and a chest of drawers were the only other items of furniture. A rag rug lay on the bare wood of the floor.

Dorrie stripped the bed and put the bedclothes in a pile to take away and wash when there was a fine drying day. Then, opening the bottom drawer of the chest she looked to see what it held. There was nothing more than everyday clothes. The rest were the same except for the two small top ones. In one of them she found gloves, handkerchiefs and other small items. There was also a trinket box. She took it out and opened it. A couple of brooches, a necklace and several rings nestled on a bed of cotton wool. Taking the box close to the window to look at them, the jewels, lit by the sun, winked and blinked at her and Dorrie was mesmerised. Were they diamonds? Where had they come from? She had no doubt that her father hadn't presented them to her mother, so who had? It was a puzzle and there was no one to help her find the answer.

But it was no good wasting time wondering so she put the box back and from the chest she took underwear, socks, stockings and everyday items of her mother's clothes that would never be worn again. She would donate the best of them to a jumble sale. That done she turned to the blanket box. Laying the rag rug on the floor in front of it she knelt on it and raised the lid.

She took out more clothes and a blanket and put them on the floor beside the box. A piece of cloth had been spread over the next layer and was tucked in all around it. She pulled that out and discovered more clothes. But these were not the sort that Dorrie had ever seen her mother wear. Dresses with waists low on the hips, beaded and embroidered and neatly folded. There were elbow length silk gloves, sheer stockings and two pairs of shoes. None of this apparel was suited to the life of a countrywoman. And once again the question was - where had they come from? And why were they there? She leaned in and took the last of the dresses out of the box and found an exercise book, the sort used in schools, hidden beneath it.

She picked it up and opened it expecting to see her own handwriting. There was writing but not hers, not a child's scrawl, but a neat adult hand. It was her mother's. She began to read.

My darling Dorothea,

By the time you read this I shall be dead and gone. But I can't go without telling you something about the sort of home I came from. Now that you have uncovered the clothes that I couldn't bear to part with you will have realized that I was not of peasant stock. No, my dear, I came from a very wealthy family who lived in a large house with an estate of many acres. It was expected that I would marry a titled man, but I fell in love with the boy who came to tend the horses. He was never a great talker but he had the most wonderful smile and I loved him. But then my father discovered that I was creeping out to the stables to meet him and though Reuben and I had done no wrong my parents threw me out and refused to pay Reuben the wages he was due. I was disinherited and was lucky to get away with a suitcase full of clothes, not that they were ever much use to me. Silk gloves are no good when you are picking up potatoes and mud does terrible things to satin shoes. I did think that if we were ever destitute I could sell the jewellery, but, thank God, it never came to that.

Your father was not always a silent, dour man. He was patient and long suffering with my lack of knowledge of country ways, but with his help and encouragement I learned how to cope with my new life. I have tried to pass on to you all the things he taught me as well as what I learned to do myself.

I have not told you who my parents were because I would not like to think that you might try to find them. Be happy in the life that has been carved out for you. Be good and kind as you have always been and one day you will find a man who will be good and kind to you.

I send love and blessings to you, my darling daughter.

Isobel Bartlett.

Chapter 6

Susan smiled as she watched her new assistant. Dorrie was an intelligent girl who never had to be told twice what to do. She was adept at understanding the complexities of rationing and ration books, a puzzlement that had Susan scratching her head. The girl's manner was always pleasant, the customers liked her, and Susan blessed the day she had asked Dorrie to come to her. It was a beneficial arrangement for them both. She was able to buy vegetables that were really fresh and Dorrie had a ready market for her produce. The added bonus of a free dinner for Dorrie had paid off and Susan smiled to see how the girl had blossomed from a skinny teenager to a rounded young woman. She was pretty and deserved to have some happiness in her life. The only child of elderly parents, Dorrie had led such an isolated existence that meeting people, old and young, was probably the reason she appeared to be so happy and relaxed these days.

It was lunch time and Susan was about to turn the sign on the door to Closed when Freda Plowman came bursting in. 'Oh Susan, you can't help me can you?' she gasped. 'You can't find me a spare bit of cheese can you? The dog's eaten mine?' Susan, her hand holding the sign, said, 'For goodness sake woman, no, I can't. This is not the first time you've come to me with a tale like that. You're not the only one whose food is rationed. You should take more care and not leave anything out where the dog can get at it.'

'Oh, but me husband does like a bit of cheese with his onion. Oh please, Susan. He'll be mad at me if he doesn't have his cheese.''

'You can have my share,' said Dorrie.

Freda Plowman beamed. 'I knew you was a good girl,' she said. 'Saved my bacon you have. My Frank would have been mad at me for days. You couldn't blame him though, could you?'

Sue Jolliffe let go of the closed sign and went back to the counter. She looked at Dorrie. 'Are you sure about this?' she said. 'It's precious little you get; you don't want to deprive yourself.'

'It's not the only source of protein, Mrs Jolliffe. I shan't come to any harm.'

'Well, as long as you're sure. Here you are then, Freda,' said Susan as she handed the woman a portion of cheese. 'But *don't* let it happen again. Put it out of reach of the dog.'

'Oh, I will, I will. Thank you, Susan, and you, Dorrie.'

'How's Garnet getting on? Have you had any news of him?' asked Susan. 'Surely he should be due some more leave, shouldn't he?'

Freda grabbed for the chair that stood beside the counter and sat down. 'Oh dear, I thought you knew. He's in France . . . well, he was.' She sniffed and swallowed. 'And he won't be coming home.' Freda took a long deep breath. 'I had a telegram to say he's missing. Presumed dead, they said. Why should I believe that? I don't think he is . . . well, I know he isn't. I *know*. I had a letter from him only yesterday.'

'My dear soul, oh Freda that's dreadful news, I'm so sorry . . .' began Susan. '*Dorrie*,' she yelled as Dorrie collapsed into a crumpled heap on the floor beside her.

'What's the matter with her?' Freda was off the chair and leaning over the counter to see what was going on.

'She's fainted. Don't just stand there gawping, run to the kitchen and get me a glass of water.' On her knees Susan slid an arm round Dorrie and lifted her up to a sitting position.

'Is she not well?' asked Freda when she came back with the water.

'I didn't think there was anything wrong with her, but I don't know. She's never done this before. Come, my dear, take a little drop of this,' said Susan as Dorrie opened her eyes.

'What . . . what happened?' asked Dorrie.

'It's nothing to worry about,' said Susan. 'You fainted, that's all. How are you feeling now? Can you stand up?' While Susan kept an arm round her Dorrie got to her feet. 'Hold on to the counter while you get back the feeling in your legs.'

Dorrie clung to the counter and leaned against it.

'My dear girl, you're white as a sheet. Come on, I'm going to take you into the back room and make you a cup of tea,' said Susan.

'Is she all right?' asked Freda.

'She will be when I've got a hot drink into her. You didn't want anything else did you?' When Freda Plowman shook her head Susan said, 'Thanks Freda, shut the door on your way out, will you?'

'Wait,' said Dorrie. 'What was that you said about Garnet?'

'Garnet. Oh, I had a telegram,' said Freda. 'They said that he was missing. They think he's dead, but I don't think he is and I'm not going to believe that 'til I feel it in here.' Freda patted her chest. 'In my heart I know he's alive and I'll only believe he's dead when I see him lying cold before me.'

'You're being very brave, Freda,' said Susan.

'It's not being brave, Susan. It's this bit in here,' Freda patted her chest again, 'that won't let me believe he's dead. It's always told me right. But I know what you mean; we all have to put on a brave front, don't we? They take our men away while we have to stay at home and pray that they'll come back to us. I believe that Garnet will come home one day and that's what you have to believe too, Dorrie Bartlett.'

'I'll do my best, Mrs Plowman,' said Dorrie.

'Well I'd better be off or Frank'll be home and if there's no dinner I'll be in trouble.'

When the shop door shut behind Freda Plowman, with an arm round Dorrie, Susan led her into the kitchen and sat her down while she made tea.

'I don't take sugar,' said Dorrie when she saw her employer spoon some into a mug.

'Yes you do,' said Susan. She poured tea, a mug for Dorrie then one for herself. Then she sat down and looked at the girl. 'You really do care for Garnet, don't you? But he's your first love, isn't he? You're taking it very seriously. Do you think that's wise?'

'I can't help it, Mrs Jolliffe. He's kind and funny and I love him.'

'But that's no reason to faint when there's bad news. It makes me think there's more to it than that he's just a boyfriend. Is there something you'd like to tell me?'

'No, I don't think so.'

Susan Jolliffe gave Dorrie a searching look. 'I do,' she said. 'There's usually a reason why people faint and I'm thinking that you did because of what Freda Plowman said and the fact that you're expecting, because you are, aren't you?'

Dorrie's hands trembled as she put her mug back on the table.

'Yes, I am. Are you going to sack me?'

'Why would I want to do that? I need you here and just because you're going to have a baby there's no reason why you can't go on working. Cheer up, it's not the end of the world.'

'But I'm not married, what will people say?'

'Quite a lot if I know the folks in this village, but you're not the first and you won't be the last. This war will see many more young unmarried women in the same condition as you. I guess that Garnet is the father and that it was what Freda said that made you faint.'

'I love him, Mrs Jolliffe. But if he . . . if he . . .' Tears gleamed in Dorrie's eyes. 'If he isn't going to come back I won't ever see him again and he doesn't know about the baby.' Dorrie's words petered off. 'We were going to get married when he had some leave. Now it's not going to happen.'

'You don't know that. The telegram Freda got didn't say he was dead. I don't think you've lost him, at least not yet, but even if you have you will have the baby. And that's got to be part of him, hasn't it?'

'They were all leaving me, Mrs Jolliffe. Mum and dad and then Garnet, and there's no more family that I know of. I took a chance with Garnet because I thought it would be all right. And it was only the once.'

'Once is enough, Dorrie. I would have thought you'd have known that.'

'But that's not true. You know that I was late coming into the world. My mother said that it wasn't for the want of trying, so once was not enough to get me born.'

'I must admit that you're right there, but that's as maybe, you'll still have a job here and we'll cope with things as they happen.'

'And if Garnet doesn't come back,' Dorrie smiled and put her hand on her stomach, 'at least I'll have this one.'

For one so young, thought Susan, to have a baby without a husband to support her was not going to be easy. Unmarried mothers were looked on unkindly and shunned. Was Dorrie aware of what she was going to have to cope with?

'Freda is convinced her boy will come home,' said Susan. 'I don't think you should give up on Garnet either. He could have been cut off from his unit. He could be quite safe somewhere but can't get word out that he is. They've only told Freda they *think* he's dead. *She's* not going to believe it and neither should you.' The shop bell tinkled. 'Oh dear, I forgot to put the closed sign up and now somebody's in the shop. You stay here, I'll go.'

Chapter 7

The war will soon be over they'd said. Yea right, pull the other one thought Garnet. He'd been a soldier for just seven months, he was in France and it was April. And why was he here? Oh yes, hc knew didn't he, he was here to fight the Germans. It hadn't been too bad at first, it was the Germans who were in retreat and the Brits were fighting them back to where they came from. He, Garnet, hadn't been in the front line but all the same mortar fire and gunshot often reached him and his mates. It had put an edge to their nerves and made it difficult to keep up a bold front. But then some wit would come out with something outrageous and laughter would cover the moment.

But things had changed and the fighting wasn't going well. The Hun had turned about and was beating them back towards the coast. Sleep was a rare commodity, a few minutes snatched here and there and Garnet was weary right through to his bones.

It was early in the day and there was dew on the grass. Daisies and other small flowers dared to hold up their heads and spring flowers were beginning to open. Trees were bursting into bud. Garnet thought of home, picnics by the river, making daisy chains for the girls. He thought of the day he had taken Dorrie for a picnic. She had been so shy and he had teased her. They would go again when he got home. They'd drink cider and eat paste sandwiches and throw the crusts to the ducks. He'd make a daisy chain for her and hold a buttercup under her chin to see if she liked butter. And he'd take her to the woods when the bluebells flowered just to see the wonder in her eyes.

The rat-tat-tat of a machine gun shattered the dream. The heavier crump of something bigger added its voice. Gerry was throwing everything at them. How could you fight a war when you were trying to get away from it? Armoured vehicles and men on foot were moving back and away from the front. But retreating was not as easy as just walking away. With his rifle in his hand Garnet's place was with his platoon. They were part of the rear guard; someone had to defend the backs of those in retreat.

'Don't they ever give up?' Barry Timmins crouched beside Garnet. 'What I'd give for a fag right now.'

'No good looking at me,' said Garnet. 'I haven't got any.'

The roar of a German plane and the whine as it dived made Garnet throw himself down beside a truck that had been abandoned.

'Move over mate.' Private Barry Timmins landed with a thump beside Garnet. 'Sod this bloody war. I've had enough of it. I really could do with fag. You sure you haven't got one?''

'No, I haven't, you already asked and I told you I didn't so shut up.'

'Miserable bastard.'

'For God's sake Timmins this is not a picnic.'

Garnet's heart ached, his body ached, his arms and his legs ached, and his feet hurt. He wanted clean socks; most of all he wanted clean socks. Why couldn't he have clean socks? It wasn't right, he shouldn't be here, none of them should. They had to move on, they had to get out, and all that bloody Timmins wanted was a fag. Didn't he know that lighting one was an invitation to the enemy to shoot him? How many more of his mates was he going to lose? How many more times was he going to see death claim them? War was an abomination and it was messing with his head.

I don't want to be here, I want to go home. I'm a farm boy. They made me a soldier, taught me how to fire a gun and kill. And the ones they want me to kill are people like me, farmers, carpenters, shop keepers. They've turned me into a murderer and murderer's burn in hell. Oh God, help me.

'Garnet, hey come on, we've got to get moving.' Corporal Jack Barker kicked at Garnet's boot. 'Come on lad; wake up, don't let it get to you - you too, Bernie.'

The explosion of a shell landing close and gunfire made them duck for cover.

'They're going to get us, Garnet,' cried Bernie Lewis. 'We're all going to die. I don't want to die.'

'You're not going to die, Bernie, shut up.'

The plane circled and came back. Bullets peppered the truck and found its petrol tank. The blast of its explosion roared through Garnets head. A tongue of flame seared his arm, ate the stuff of his sleeve, his trouser leg, and cooked his flesh, burned his face and his hair. Fragments of jagged metal flew through the air. Garnet rolled in the grass. Thank God for the dew. Snatching off his helmet he rubbed at his hair. Pain clutched the burns that blistered on his leg, his arm, his face, his hands. Pain was a torment, a torture and like nothing he'd known before. Pain devoured him, dulled his senses and took away knowledge of time and place.

'Mum,' he cried. 'Where are you mum?'

Stinking of burnt cloth and the mess in his pants Garnet collapsed, lay on his back and stared at the sky.

'Somebody, anybody, help - help me,' cried a voice.

'Who's that?'

'Is that you Garnet? It's me Bernie.'

Little Bernie, apple of his mother's eye, not very bright, but fit and able to fire a gun, he too had been dragged to the battlefield and taught how to kill.

'What's wrong, we've got to get going,' said Garnet to Bernie's prone figure. 'Get up and follow me.'

'Can't, I got no legs.'

'What d'you mean, you got no legs?'

'Can't feel em, they aren't there.'

Garnet stuck the butt of his gun in the ground and used it to support him while he leaned over Bernie. Bernie reached up grabbed hold of and held tight to the front of Garnet's tunic.

'I'm going to die, Garnet. I don't want to die,' he whined.

'Don't be daft, Bernie.'

'I am. I know I am. Me mam was here.'

'What?'

'She came to take me home. But I'm going to die.' Bernie's grasp on Garnet lessened. 'Tell her, Garnet. When you get home tell her you seen me.'

'Tell her yourself, Bernie.'

'I'm going to die, Garnet. I'm afraid. It'll be dark, Garnet.'

'No it won't, it'll be like a summer's day.' Tears filled Garnet's eyes. Where was the sense in war?

Bernie's grip slackened, 'I don't . . . like,' he lost it and fell back. '. . . the dark.'

Bernie was dead.

A slow anger began to burn in Garnet. Everyone back home knew Bernie's mother. Deserted by the man she had been going to marry she had struggled to raise Bernie on her own, and now she had to lose him too. He closed the boy's eyes, whispered 'God rest your soul,' then, hauling himself to his feet, stood and turned away.

Where are the others? Where's Jack? Got to get moving, go on, go on. Save yourself. No, find Jack. He's over there, go and look. It looks like he's sleeping, not with his eyes open though. Ah but he is, he's sleeping the sleep that he'll never wake up from. Oh God, too late to do anything for Jack. Garnet closed his eyes and tried mentally to overcome his anguish, his agony, it was a losing battle. Exhaustion and the pain of his burns was too much, he collapsed and slipped into oblivion.

The exodus went on without Garnet. Troops moved on towards the coast leaving casualties and the dead to be picked up by those only God knew. Day slid by, daylight faded, leaving the darkness of night broken only by a rising moon. How long he had lain there Garnet did not know, but he began to stir when rain started to fall. Except for sporadic gunfire which was some distance away all was eerily quiet. Although his burns still stung he was alive. He had to get away. He pulled himself to his feet.

'Timmins, Timmins, where are you, come on we've got to go,' he croaked.

When Timmins did not reply Garnet looked for him, found him by the side of the truck. For a second or two Garnet gazed on the shattered body of a man who had no face but did have a jagged piece of metal buried deep in his chest. Turning away he vomited, retched until his stomach was empty. Retched again and again until he thought his stomach was going to follow its contents.

With the loss of daylight there was a lull in the fighting and the sound of battle had faded. Vehicles and men of his battalion had moved on and left him among the dead. He had to join them if he was going to get away, get home or at least find a place of safety. Uncertain which way to go he looked to the sky. The moon, as did the sun, rose in the east. He needed to go west. Should he follow the road or would it double back on itself and make the journey twice as long? Roads tended to do that. No, he would go across country. It would be safer. Using his rifle as a makeshift crutch he began to walk. Every movement was a separate agony. The fringes of the burnt cloth of his uniform rubbed against the raw flesh of his burns. The seared skin of his face wept and ran down his neck. But he wasn't going to give up. He had to survive, had to try to find his company, had to be on the transport home.

The rain that had been falling like a blessing became intense, fell hard and struck with spite. The ground that had been winter soft became a quagmire.

As he started on his journey Garnet did his best to shake off the distress of witnessing the separate deaths of Bernie, of Jack, and of Barry Timmins. If he ever did get home he would have to see Bernie's mother and lie about the bravery of her son. What else could he do?

There was a voice then. A shadowy voice that whined, 'Don't leave me, Garnet. Let me come with you, Garnet.'

Timmins, Barry Timmins. No, it couldn't be. Barry was dead. A quick look over the shoulder and there he was, a grey figure, faceless, following him. Press on, press on. Don't look back.

Three Germans in long grey coats confronted him now. They grinned at him.

'Where are you going, English? You cannot win. We shall get you.'

'Get out of my way.' No time to fire the gun. Use it like a stick, swing it. It's heavy. The gun sliced through empty air. Garnet lost his balance and fell in the mud. The German's laughed and faded away.

There were bodies on the ground, twisted, shapeless bodies. Not all were dead. They called out as he passed. 'Help, Help.' But he could not.

What agony was this? Why are men dying in a bed of mud?

'Wait, Garnet. Wait for us.' Timmins again, and Bernie, too, and with them the writhing, lurching, swaying grey forms of the dead. Garnet upped his pace. Had to get away - had to get away.

Rain had softened the skin over his burns and the pain was less. He began to run, not fast, hopping with his good leg, trying to rest the one that was burnt. Faster and faster and still the grey ghosts of men were behind him. They were keeping up with him. They would not leave him. He could not shake them off and still he could hear the mocking laughter of the Germans.

Run, Garnet, run. Run for your life.

The rifle, clogged with mud, was an impediment. It was no use. He threw it away. Losing the burden gave wings to his feet. He could run faster now. For the first time he felt a twinge of happiness. He was going home.

Suddenly the ground sloped away under him. The surface of the embankment was wet. He slipped.

He fell.

He rolled.

Bushes scratched and whipped him. Stones and rocks bit him. A ditch caught him. And then the deep dark swallowed him.

Chapter 8

'Now young lady,' said Susan Jolliffe. 'You are going to come and stay with me to have your baby. I will never be able to sleep at night if I think you are giving birth all on your own. Now promise me you will.'

Dorrie smiled. 'All right, but there's quite a long time before it's due so I'm not going to come yet. I'd rather be at home with Moss.'

Susan put a hand on Dorrie's arm. 'But Moss isn't going to be much good when you go into labour.'

'No I know she won't, but stop worrying, I won't leave it that late.'

'All right then. Now I don't want to upset you . . . but I don't suppose *you've* had any word from Garnet, have you?'

'No, I haven't. You heard what his mother said; the army believe he's dead. I don't know what's happened to him, but there's nothing I can do about it so I just have to carry on as normal.'

'You're a brave girl. But any time you've got a problem come to me, if I can't sort it out we'll find someone who can.' She smiled at Dorrie. 'Come on then, we've got work to do.'

Dorrie weighed up sugar, ounces of butter, quartered cheese and cut coupons out of ration books. The cheery face she presented while she worked and served the customers was hard to maintain at times. Especially when some sour faced spinster made disparaging remarks about the loose morals of young women. Invariably the remark that 'it was not like it in my day' was quickly parried by Susan Jolliffe who said that that was nonsense because it had always been the same, it was just that hooped petticoats were better at covering up than today's fashions were. There was an end to it and she didn't want to hear that sort of talk in the shop again.

It was different for Dorrie when she was at home. Her expanding girth and the weight she carried made her tired, and standing behind the shop counter for much of the day did not help. When there were but a few weeks to go to her confinement she gave up work. She tired easily so only did what was essential. On good days she sat on a bench by the back wall of her house - a rough wooden bench that her father had made - and enjoyed the balmy weather. Moss went with her everywhere. When Dorrie sat on the bench the dog lay at her feet.

When July was running out of days Dorrie packed a bag. In it she put all the little garments she had made or bought for her baby. She bundled up nappies, pins and powder then added a tiny hairbrush and rattle, knew it was too soon for them, but she had been unable to resist when she saw them in the shop. She also put in clothes for herself. Not much; she didn't plan to stay away from home for long. And then she let Susan Jolliffe know that she was ready. Moss was to stay with Rosie and her little ones.

The day before Reg Jolliffe came to pick her up Dorrie spent the afternoon sitting in the garden. From where she sat she could see it and nearly all of the paddocks. She had not been able to do anything out of doors for several weeks and saw how weeds were taking over. She salvaged green peas and ate them straight from the pod. She picked broad beans, cooked them, put a knob of her precious butter ration on them and enjoyed them. The fruit on the blackcurrant bushes could be reached from where she sat. She leaned forward, picked and ate them, and stained her mouth with the rich red juice.

*

Lucas James Bartlett was born at eight am on Friday the 9th of August. He bawled loudly when he came into the world and Dorrie wondered if it was by way of greeting or in protest at what she had just put him through.

The midwife laughed. 'He's got a good pair of lungs. He'll be a singer.'

'That's good,' said Dorrie, 'for I can't sing a note.'

Susan Jolliffe, who had been beside Dorrie throughout the girl's labour, was hard pressed to hold back her tears of joy. 'You'll never be alone again my dear,' she said. 'This one is going to fill your days with happiness.'

When Dorrie had been settled and the baby washed and dressed and lying in her arms, Susan said, 'Don't you think someone ought to tell Garnet's mother she has a grandson? She does know that Garnet is your baby's father, doesn't she?'

'Well *I* haven't told her.'

'The village probably has. But we ought to let her know, don't you think?'

'I'll tell her,' said the midwife. 'I pass her house on my way home. I'll pop in again this evening to see how you're doing, Dorrie. Enjoy your baby.'

'We shall have to find a pram from somewhere,' said Susan. 'I ought to have thought about that before. I'll put a notice in the shop window, though I may still have my old one. And what about a cot, have you got anything to . . . why, whatever is the matter?'

Dorrie's head was bent over her baby. Tears coursed down her face. 'It's all wrong,' she said. 'My mother and father aren't here and Garnet ought to be. I've no family and Lucas won't have a father. Folk will think the worst of me. I've got a child and I'm not married.'

Silent tears turned to sobs. Susan took the girl into her arms and Dorrie buried her face in Susan's ample bosom.

'Hush now,' said Susan. 'You made a rash decision, but having to part from someone you love not knowing if you'll ever see them again means that people do that. It also means that you have to accept the consequences. We none of us know what life is going to dish out for us, but whatever it is we just have to get on with it. And if I know you that is what you will do. I'll always be here for you and when you're ready you can come back to work and bring the little one with you. Now let's have a smile.'

'You're so kind to me.'

'Dry your eyes then while I go and get you a cup of tea.'

Alone with her baby, Dorrie opened up the shawl he was wrapped in. Gently she examined his little body, marvelled over tiny hands and feet, stroked his soft black hair. He opened his eyes and looked at her.

'Hello darlin',' she said and wrapped him up again. 'Welcome to the world. It's not the nicest place at the moment, but we'll be all right.'

Footsteps on the stairs and the murmur of voices announced the arrival of Susan and Freda Plowman. Susan carried a tray with tea for Dorrie.

'I hope you're not cross with me, Mrs Plowman,' said Dorrie.

'Cross, why should I be when you've given me a grandson? Let me look at him.'

'Don't just look, why don't you hold him?'

'Sit here, Freda,' said Susan, 'and give him a cuddle while Dorrie has a drink.'

Freda Plowman crooned to the baby in her arms, rocked him back and forth, kissed him and cuddled him. Then she sat still and for a long minute studied him. A stray tear crept down her cheek. 'There's no doubt at all about who his father is,' she said. 'He looks just like Garnet did as a baby. I *know* he will come home again . . . and I don't like to say it . . . but if he doesn't at least we have a little bit of him here.'

'He is going to come home. I'm sure of it,' said Dorrie.

'Yes, of course. And so am I. Until we're told that he won't come back we have to believe that he will. Can I come and see . . . what's the baby's name?'

'I thought Lucas James would be nice. What do you think?'

'I like it. But I'd better give him back to you and get going; I've got things to do.' Freda put the baby back in Dorrie's arms and kissed her. 'Let me know if there's anything you need that I can get for you and I'll see what I can do. And don't fret. Garnet will come back to us one day.'

'I must go too,' said Susan. 'Let me put the baby down to sleep and you have a sleep as well, Dorrie. I'll come up and see you later on.'

Chapter 9

Pushed back to the shores of France, what was left of the British Expeditionary Force had been rescued from Dunkirk. Now the Germans were attacking Britain. The Luftwaffe bombed London, other cities, airfields and docks. The attacks were merciless. A continuous rain of bombs was dropped on people and buildings alike. Whole streets of houses were razed. Those who lived in cities and built up areas spent their nights in air raid shelters or on the platforms in underground stations. It was not comfortable but it was safe. They emerged in the morning not knowing what they were to find. Would their homes be standing or no more than a pile of rubble?

Susan Jolliffe listened to the radio and wrung her hands in despair. 'Thank goodness we live in the country,' she said when she relayed the news to Dorrie. 'They're not going to attack a village. It's the airfields and the factories they're aiming for. It would have to be a stray bomb to hit us. I don't think that's likely to happen but you never know. Bristol's just north of us and I'm sure I've heard planes going that way. Southampton's south and they go for both of them. She looked at Dorrie and at the pram in the corner of the shop. That girl ought not to live alone.

'You know, Dorrie . . .' Susan began.

'No, don't even think about it,' said Dorrie when she saw the look Susan gave her. 'You were going to say I ought not to be living alone, but it's not likely we'll get bombed so Luc and I are staying at Leanacres.'

'I wish you wouldn't. There's always room for you here.' They were weighing up sugar rations. 'London got bombed again last night, the docks as well. I lie awake sometimes and listen. You can hear the throb of the bombers engines when they fly over. I hope you keep your door locked.'

'We never used to, but I do now. But a locked door isn't going to stop a bomb so stop worrying, Susan.'

'I don't care. I still think you ought not to be up there on your own. A young woman like you should be with a family.'

Dorrie shrugged. 'But that's just it. I haven't got one.'

'No, and more's the pity.' Susan Jolliffe stood arms akimbo, hands on her ample hips. She turned away and began tidying the top of the counter. 'Why don't you stay and have supper with us tonight? I hate to think of you up there all on your own night after night.'

'Thank you, I'd like that.'

*

Supper in the Jolliffe's house was a substantial meal. Dorrie looked on in surprise when Susan put a casserole on the table along with a dish of boiled potatoes and another of beans. When had she had time to cook all this? Or was the preparation of it the reason she left Dorrie in the shop on her own from time to time, and was this why she needed an assistant? Whatever it was here on the table was what made Susan's figure 'comfortable', her husband's the same.

'Come, sit down and eat,' said Susan as she dished up. 'And help yourself to vegetables.'

Dorrie began to add potatoes to the plate of food Susan had given her. Reg had poured himself a glass of beer.

'Don't stint yourself, girl,' he said to Dorrie when he saw the small amount of food on her plate. 'There's plenty of veg and it looks to me as though you could do with a good meal. You need feeding up.'

'Leave her alone, Reg, she knows what she wants.'

When the meal was finished and the washing up done Susan insisted that Dorrie stay a while. 'There's a moon tonight, so you'll be all right going home, and Luc's sleeping so he won't care how long you stay.' She picked up her knitting bag, took out knitting needles and a ball of wool, and cast on the stitches needed to knit socks for her husband. 'Switch the radio on, Reg,' she said. 'Let's see if there's any news.'

It wasn't the news they got but Tommy Handley, and 'It's That Man Again'.

Susan laughed. 'Oh this is so funny, just what we need to cheer us up. There's that other one I like, 'Round the Horn'. You like that one too, don't you Reg? Have you got a radio yet, Dorrie?' Susan held up a hand. 'Shhh, listen. Turn the volume down, Reg.'

The radio silenced, all three concentrated on listening. To them came the drone of aircraft engines.

'They're going to Bristol,' said Susan. 'Pity the poor folk who live there.'

'I don't know how they cope with it all,' said Dorrie. 'Whatever must it be like to spend the night in a shelter and then when you come out in the morning find that your house is gone? Fancy losing the things you hold precious like photographs and letters.'

'And they're things you can never replace. Gerry's gone on now, Reg. We can listen to a bit more. Turn the sound up a bit.'

The Jolliffe's sitting room was warm and comfortable. A log fire burned in the grate. Light was provided by an electric light bulb which, surrounded by a conical shade, hung from the ceiling.

'It must be lovely to be able to turn the light on by just clicking a switch,' said Dorrie. 'Much more convenient than having to remember to fill the lamp with oil and to trim the wick like I have to. I don't suppose electricity will ever get to Leanacres.'

'Never say never,' said Susan. 'I am constantly amazed at the changes that have taken place in my lifetime.' Sitting back in her chair she finished the row of knitting she was doing and was in the act of changing over the needles when a loud thump from somewhere outside made her jump. 'Oh my God, what was that?' she cried.

An even louder thump was followed by a deafening roar that filled the room. Walls vibrated, pictures chattered.

'What's that? It sounds like a train,' cried Susan.

'I think it's an aircraft,' said Reg.

An aircraft it was, directly overhead, flying much too low, its engines labouring. The house shook. Then it was gone. Seconds later came the muffled sound of an explosion. Susan threw down her knitting, Reg his paper, Dorrie a piece of sewing that was in her hand.

'It's the Germans,' cried Susan.

'Don't be daft,' said Reg.

Susan was making for the door, 'I'm going to see,' she said.

'Now I know she is. Come on Dorrie,' said Reg as he followed his wife.

In the street the feeble light given by torches showed up like glow-worms. Men were shouting and running. Women stood looking out of their houses.

'Hey you,' Susan called to a man going by. 'What's going on?'

'One of the Gerry planes has been shot down. We think it's crashed on the common.'

'Oh my God, my house?' cried Dorrie.

Abandoning friends and baby, she ran. No hat, no coat and no cares for either, Dorrie ran. Her house was on the common, her possessions, her memories and her life. Regardless of men who were running too, Dorrie sprinted past them. Then Reg Jolliffe was there with his car. He threw the door open. 'Get in,' he shouted and Dorrie, in haste and gasping for breath, fell in to the passenger seat.

As they neared Leanacres they could see the roof of the cottage outlined against the red glow of a fire that was coming from somewhere beyond it. Even before Reg had stopped the car Dorrie had the door open and was jumping out. Other vehicles were pulling up and more men, soldiers and even PC Roberts were there. Reg grabbed Dorrie's arm to hold her back when she made to join them and go to where the plane had crashed.

'You don't know what might happen. There may be other bombs still on board. I can't risk you getting killed. You've got Luc to think about. You haven't lost your house. Everything seems to be all right here. Let's go home. We'll hear all about it tomorrow.'

'No, I want to see,' said Dorrie, and despite his exhortations that she should not Reg could do nothing but go with her.

'Stand back, stand back,' said a man as they drew near. 'You don't want to get too close, it's dangerous.'

Reg Jolliffe held firmly to Dorrie's arm and kept her close to his side while they stood to watch as fire ate the crumpled mess that had been a plane.

'I wonder if the crew got out,' said Dorrie. 'They do bail out, don't they?'

'They can if they're not too low, but I believe the pilot, like a ship's captain, stays with his plane.'

'So is there a dead man in there? Oh how awful. I don't want to stay any longer, let's go.'

Later that evening as she walked back to Leanacres with Luc tucked up in the pram, Dorrie was in a thoughtful mood. At the entrance to the common she pushed the pram through the gateway and let the gate fall to. Moss was there waiting for her. Dorrie smiled, bent to caress the dog and walked on.

Until that night, apart from shortages, food rationing and the absence of young men, war seemed to be taking place far, far away from Monkton Priors. But now bombs had been dropped, jettisoned by a plane about to crash. Rumour was that they had fallen on Dickie Brigg's farm, killed some of his cows and left craters in his home meadow. The plane had made its last contact with land, a fatal crash in which men had died, and because of it the reality of war had been brought home to the residents of the village.

Dorrie thought of Garnet and of the troops that had been picked up from French beaches, rescued from the assault of Hitler's army and brought home. Garnet should have come with them. Where was he? Although Dorrie tried hard to convince herself that he would come home there were so many possibilities of what might have happened to him that she could find no answer.

If all the news they were given was correct the Germans had inflicted terrible things on the French. War was not the glorious winning of a battle; it was a senseless killing of men, the snuffing out of life. To Dorrie it made no sense at all for it was now spring and the earth was doing what it always did, bursting into life again, pushing the green spears of plants up and into rain and wind and the sun and dressing the trees in their new clothes. It was not a time to die.

'Come now, my beauty,' she said to her dog as she took a key from her bag and unlocked her door. 'You've waited for me for hours so now it's time for you.' She pushed the pram inside and made room for it beside the table. 'Here you are, Moss,' she said as she put down a dish of food.

Chapter 10

At the shop Dorrie hung up her coat and put on her apron, ready to start work.

'We shall have a lot of customers today, but we shall sell nothing. Everybody will be talking about that plane crash,' said Susan. 'Reg said there wasn't much to see last night and that you and he weren't allowed to go near.'

'Quite right too,' said Dorrie. 'Things were going pop and bang and burning stuff was spitting out all over the place. When I thought that men might have been burned alive inside that plane my blood ran cold.'

Susan unlocked the shop door and turned the sign to OPEN. 'Oh dear,' she said, 'they haven't wasted any time. Stand by for here they come.'

'Did you hear all that kerfuffle last night, Susan?' said Freda Plowman as she burst into the shop. 'It's a mercy them bombs weren't dropped on us or we would all be dead.'

'Did you want something, Freda?'

'Oh no, Susan, I just come to hear what you thought about it all. One of them bombs killed three of Dickie Brigg's cows.'

'Yes,' piped up another, 'and now he's got two great big holes in the meadow close to home where he had none. They bombs only just missed his house they say.'

'I tell you, I was feared for my life,' said Freda. 'I thought that plane was going to take the roof off, the noise it made was awful.'

'Makes you wonder how our men get on with bombs dropping all round them and soldiers firing at them,' said the woman Freda came in with.

'Shush,' said a woman to a child that was tugging at her hand. 'No you can't have any sweeties I haven't got any coupons left.' She turned her attention to the rest of the gathering. 'It's all very well,' she said. 'We do nothing but complain because we think we're hard done by. We're lucky that the bombs didn't drop on us, but what about our men? I don't like to think what they've got to go through. We ought to be able to do something to help, but God only knows what.'

'Can you knit?' asked Dorrie.

'Knit, course I can, what's that got to do with it?'

'You could knit comforts for the troops. They need warm socks and gloves and, well, you know.'

'Huh,' said the woman. 'And where would I get the wool? I unravel jumpers and re-knit them for the kids as it is. You got to give coupons for new wool.'

'The WVS organises things like that,' said Dorrie. 'I could get in touch with them and see what they can do? That's if you would be interested, of course.'

'I would,' said the woman and, 'I would,' said Freda.

'Okay, I'll see them next time I go into town,' said Dorrie.

'You've started something now,' said Susan, and, 'Now then you lot,' to the gossiping women, 'if you don't want to buy anything get along home and let me and Dorrie get on.'

For several more days little knots of women gathered in the shop to talk about the crash, to wonder what they'd do about it if there was ever another. Some said they would use their husband's shot gun and shoot any German that threatened her or her family. Some said they would lock doors and windows and let the army deal with it. Most said that it was an event that was never likely to happen again, and little by little the subject was dropped. Gradually interest in the village's taste of war died down and it dropped back into its sleepy state, almost, but not quite. So many things in daily use such as hair pins and grips, even shampoo, were unobtainable. The leather soles of shoes were replaced with wood. In the shops the first of the American troops confused staff by asking for thumb tacks when they meant drawing pins. They spoke English, but with a difference. In spite of it all the day by day work went back to its usual routine. Telling Susan that lightning never struck the same place twice, Dorrie continued to live at Leanacres and to walk to and from work each day.

Home after a long and tiring day Dorrie lit the fire, filled the kettle and hung it on the pot hook then set bread and jam, a plate, a mug and the teapot on the table. She stirred the fire, fed Lucas then began to eat while she waited for the kettle to boil. When it did and after she had eaten she settled her baby down to sleep.

Not wanting to leave him in the house while she went into the garden to relax after the day's work she took him with her and parked the pram beside Reuben's bench where she would sit and unwind. She had not been able to spend much time in the garden since her baby had been born and her absence had, as ever, given the weeds a chance to take advantage. It badly needed attention. But not inclined to garden that eveningm and because the sun shone on the back of the house and warmed the wall, there she sat on the bench. The vegetable garden lay in front of her. Two large plots were divided by a dirt path that led to a small gate which opened on to the common land.

Beyond the stream at the bottom of the valley the land was rough. Rushes and tussocks of dead grass denoted bog. Beyond that again was more rough ground before it terminated in an area of woodland in which moss laden trees were half hidden by a thick undergrowth of shrubs, ivy, bryony and brambles. At the edge of the wood, willows, revelling in the wet, boggy ground, waved their slim branches and crept ever closer to the stream.

Dorrie relaxed, leaned back against the wall, and looked up at small clouds that hung motionless in the sky. She watched as rooks, talking noisily to one another, flapped their way back to their roosts in pairs. She saw the wide spread wings of a buzzard high above, watched its lazy quartering of the land beneath while its eyes and ears searched for the rustlings and movements of small mammals. She heard its cry, peeiou, peeiou. She followed its movements for a while then brought her gaze down to look towards the woods. Sometimes a deer would venture out at this time of day and make its way to the stream to drink.

The sun sank low in the west and daylight began to fade. The moon was creeping up from the horizon ready to replace the gold of sunlight with its silver. Dorrie loved this time of day; it was a time to relax after the hustle and bustle of the shop. She was about to give up and go indoors when a movement at the edge of the wood caught her eye. Perhaps deer were coming to drink. They were beautiful, graceful animals, but nervous and hesitant to show themselves. Patiently she waited.

'Come on, come on, I want to see you,' she whispered.

The undergrowth was thick. Bushes trembled, stilled. Shook again then parted to reveal . . .

Dorrie gasped. 'No . . .'

Chapter 11

A head pushed through green branches, turned slowly left and right. Paused . . . waited, then thinking that it was safe to show itself, the body to which the head belonged parted the bushes and stepped forward. Dorrie slid off the bench and crouched low behind the dark canes of black currants. The thing that had come out of the wood was not an animal, but a man.

Clad in a flying suit, trouser bottoms tucked into calf length boots, he stood partly in and partly out of the wood. Dorrie needed no telling that this must be one of the German airmen who had bailed out of the plane that had crashed. Where had he been? What had he been living on? Did he have a gun? Would he come and shoot her? She was in danger and there was no time to lose. She crawled round the corner of the house and out of his sight then ran.

She had kept her father's shotgun in a narrow cupboard next to the fireplace. It was still there. She snatched open the door. On its butt end the gun leaned into the corner of the cupboard. She picked it up, reached for the box of cartridges on the shelf above, took two and loaded them into the barrel. Hoping that she wouldn't need to use them she sent up a silent prayer thanking her father for teaching her how to shoot.

I'm taking too long, she thought. Where is the German now, what's he doing? The gun on her arm, barrel broken for safety, she crept back round the house. Moss padded silently at her heels. At the corner she stopped, took a deep breath then cautiously looked round it.

The man was about to cross the stream. Dorrie watched as he tested the plank bridge, found it firm, walked across then began to walk towards the house. She had to stop him while he was still in the open where he would be at her mercy. She could not let him get into the house or any of the buildings where he would have the advantage of her. He walked confidently and without fear. How arrogant he was. But that's what Germans were like, weren't they?

He was still too far away. She had to wait until he was within range. But what was she going to do with him when he was? Was she going to shoot him or would the sight of the gun be enough? And if she did stop him, what then, stand there all night until someone came to arrest him and rescue her? No one ever came to Leanacres unless they were asked or had business to conduct. It was not too late; she could go back and lock herself and Luc in the house.

But no, this man, an enemy of Britain, had to be stopped; there was nothing else she could do. He was closer now. It was time. Sliding round the corner of the house and glad that the dark colour of the frock she wore blended with the wall, Dorrie walked forward. But he saw her and waved a hand, even smiled. Fool. Keeping the gun close to her side she went down the garden path, kicked the gate open then clicking the barrel shut as she brought the gun up she pointed it at him and shouted, '*Stop.*'

He smiled again, shook his head, and continued to walk towards her.

Close to Dorrie's side, Moss gave a low warning growl.

She only had two cartridges. Why hadn't she put some more in her pocket? She shouted again to him to stop and when he didn't she pointed the gun in the air and fired then trained it on him again. The sudden noise woke Luc who screamed in fright.

His hands raised, the German stood still and looked at her. 'You vould not really shoot me, vould you?'

The words were English but the accent definitely German.

'Yes, I would,' said Dorrie. 'Do not take another step. Stay where you are.'

'You don't need to shoot me. I am obliged to give myself up.'

Well he might say that, but what would he do if she put the gun down?

'Walk on,' she said. 'But don't come any closer to me than you are now.'

She indicated with the barrel of the gun that he should walk round the perimeter of the garden. She followed him until they came close to the house. Telling him to stop, she reached for the handle of the pram and with one eye on her prisoner pulled it to her.

'Do I haf to keep my hands in the air?' asked the German.

'Yes you do.' Dorrie wriggled the pram around until she could push it forward. 'Now walk on,' she said, 'that way, down the road, go.'

With the butt of the gun tucked under her arm, the barrel resting in her hand, Dorrie, with a now softly whimpering baby, followed her prisoner along the track through the common gate and to the village. The street was deserted. When they reached the Lamb and Flag Dorrie called a halt and waited. Sounds of voices and laughter drifted out to her. Surely someone would look through a window, see her and come out.

'How long do ve have to vait?'

'Not a moment longer,' said Dorrie, and pointing the gun at the sky, she fired off the second cartridge. It had the desired effect.

PC Roberts, followed by a couple of soldiers and the landlord of the pub tumbled out through the door.

'My God, what are you doing, Dorrie?' asked the policeman.

'I was looking for some help because I have a prisoner for you and I wasn't going to wait 'til closing time,' she said. 'Will you take him now? I want to go home.'

*

Susan Jolliffe was taking in her washing. Picking up the basket of clothes she carried it into her kitchen. Reg, sitting with his feet up, was reading the paper.

'I just heard a gunshot,' said Susan.

'Don't be daft, Susan. Nobody would fire a gun in the village. It must have been a car backfiring.'

'No. It was definitely a shot, just one . . .' Susan gasped. 'Ooh, Reg, it's either the Germans or somebody's intent on murder and we're all going to be shot.'

'Aagh, don't be silly, Sue. You're making a fuss about nothing.' Reg Jolliffe put down his paper and stood up. 'Better go and have a look to see what's going on I suppose. Come on, you'd better come too.'

Dorrie, accompanied by PC Roberts, was on her way home and just passing the shop when the Jolliffes stepped out onto the road.

'What are you doing out at this time of night?' asked Susan.

'I had a delivery to make,' said Dorrie.

'That she did,' said PC Roberts, 'and a very important one, too. One of them German's that bailed out of that plane turned up at Leanacres. Dorrie marched him here at gun point. There's a couple of soldiers looking after him now and the Military police are coming to take him away, so I'm going to see that this young lady gets home safely.'

Chapter 12

Garnet opened his eyes and tried to raise his head. It was heavy and it hurt. He moved his hands. They were bandaged. Beneath his arms, which were bare, he felt cloth, soft, like cotton. Where was the mud? Where were the sounds of battle? He sniffed the air. It was not outdoor fresh, but warm. He was lying in a bed indoors somewhere. He sniffed again. There was a smell of something savoury, soup, or roasting meat. Someone was cooking. He was home and his mother was getting dinner. A smile spread across his face, came to a sudden stop when it hurt. Why was that?

But no, he could not be home. His mother would not have left him in the dark. Sound of movement, someone was coming. A door creaked; there was a glimmer of light and a figure bending over him. A lantern was raised and in its light he saw a face. It was not one he knew.

Cool hands and a soft voice. 'Sh, is all right, Tommy. You are safe.'

Garnet clutched the hand that held his. He looked at the woman.

'Who are you, where am I?'

'I am Michelle. You are with me. Rest now, I bring you some soup.'

As quickly as she had come she was gone.

Michelle. He knew no one of that name. Who was she and where is he? He could not be at one of the field stations where soldiers are patched up and sent back to the front or away to a hospital. Here it is dark. There they would have light, doctors and nurses and the moaning and groaning of broken men. There is none of that here. Garnet tried again to raise his head. He put his hands up to it and even though his fingers are wrapped he can tell that that his head is swathed in bandages. He tries to move his legs. One is fine, he can bend the knee, but the other is stiff. He feels his body. There is a pain in his side, belly is okay, but back, ribs and chest are tender. There is nothing for it but to lay still and wait.

The woman comes back with soup. It smells good and Garnet knows how hungry he is. She puts the bowl on a table along with her lantern then, putting her arm under the mattress he lays on, lifts it a little and pushes a cushion under it to keep it raised. As she does a sharp pain makes Garnet cry out.

'Je suis désolé, I am sorry,' she says.

Lifting the bowl she spoons soup into his mouth. He closes his eyes as he swallows. Tears gather in them as he accepts the food she has prepared. Afraid that she will leave him again, between mouthfuls of soup he reaches out to her.

'What am I doing here?

'It was not your time to die. You would not have been brought to me if it had been. Now listen. The Germans have driven the British out of France and sent them home. There was not time to send you with them so you will stay here. When you are better you will help me. You will be called Pierre, be my little brother, who is dumb. You will only speak when we are inside the house. You must speak French. If you can't you must learn.'

Garnet thought back to his schooldays and his head master, a man who wore shoes that were brown and shiny as a conker and spats that peeped out from under his trouser bottoms. Learn to speak French? Mr Jenson had enough trouble teaching his pupils to speak English. To coach them in a foreign language was out of the question.

'Why should I learn it?'

'You are not deaf so you must understand. I will teach you.'

'I know how I got this,' Garnet indicated his bandaged limbs, 'but how do you say I did?'

'Your house was hit by a bomb. There was a fire. Your wife died and you came to me. No more questions. I get you some coffee.'

Fed, watered, warm and made comfortable, Garnet relaxed and closed his eyes. Sleep came quickly and with it came bad dreams. At first the street was like any other but as he walked it became familiar. He was home. He was in the village and there was his mother coming to meet him. But someone was hanging on to his coat. Someone was pulling him back. 'It's me, Gar,' said a voice. 'You left me, Gar. You left all of us.'

A grey, nebulous shape danced around him. Timmins, Timmins without a face. Timmins with the piece of metal stuck in his chest. And there was Bernie, weeping and wailing, and there were others. The ghosts of the dead he had left behind, their broken bodies writhing, wreathing, clutched at him. He could feel their hands, soft and ill-defined like jelly, could smell their fetid breath. Bathed in sweat Garnet fought the sheets that had twisted into ropes and tied him down. Go away Timmins, go away and leave me alone. I can't help you. Go away, go away, *go away*. The voice that came next was loud. 'Private Garnet Plowman you are accused of desertion and as such you are to be shot.' His back against the wall Garnet looked at the barrels of the guns pointed at him. The guns barked and Garnet screamed. 'NOOOOOOO.'

And then Michelle was there. 'It was a nightmare, mon cher, you are here with me. You are safe.'

*

Garnet's recovery was slow. Michelle introduced him to Laurent and told him that he was the doctor who had treated his injuries. 'He is a good man,' she said.

'Then I owe my life to you,' said Garnet. 'Tell me what I can do to repay you.'

'That would depend on what skills you have,' said Laurent.

'I can garden, grow stuff. Not much else but fiddle with radio's to keep them working. It's not much to offer.'

'If I find a radio that needs repair I will bring it to you,' said Laurent.

'We need the radio,' said Michelle when Laurent had gone. 'There is nothing else in the way of entertainment. We need it for news, too.' Then she smiled a secret smile and said. 'There are also other things we need it for.' But she would not say what.

Eventually Garnet was able to sit and stand and walk without Michelle to guide him. Each day she taught him to speak French in the way she spoke it. 'You have to sound as though this is your home,' she said. 'You must learn some German, too.'

She brought him fresh clothes, not new but the sort worn by local men. 'You also have to look the part,' she said. 'I have stitched your identity tag into the hem of your coat. It needs to be hidden. It will be safe there.'

Garnet watched Michelle as she went about her tasks. She was a strong, upright and good looking woman. As to age, well that was hard to tell, but maybe forty five – fifty. She wore a wedding ring but there were no signs of a husband, no photographs to adorn the shelves or to hang on the wall. So what was she doing here alone?

She was teaching him her language when the Germans came. Arrogant and proud to have been victorious in turning the British out of France, they came with their motor cycles and trucks. They roared round the house, strode into it in their jackboots and raided Michelle's larder. They looked into cupboards and on shelves and took away eggs and potatoes and carrots and anything else they could find. They looked Garnet up and down, asked him who he was and what he was doing there and Garnet grunted and made noises that were not words and when Michelle told them he was dumb they left him alone. He prayed they would not touch Michelle for if they did he didn't know how he would be able to stop himself from attacking them. But his resolve was not to be tried for the Germans, happy with their loot, got into their trucks and on to their motor cycles and rode away.

'Have they done this before?' asked Garnet when he and Michelle counted the cost of what had been stolen.

'Yes, and it will happen again. But all is not lost. The hens will lay more eggs and the cow will give more milk and there are potatoes hidden away. They didn't get them all. But one day when they come I will shoot them and I shall enjoy it.'

'And I will help you.'

Handicapped though he was, for the skin of his burns had pulled tight, Garnet enjoyed working with Michelle. One day he would go home. He would really like to marry Dorrie, love her and care for her. But that was something he could not now do. How could he ask her to tie herself to a man with a face like his? Michelle had hidden all her mirrors and it wasn't until he had looked into the top of the water butt one day and saw his face that he knew how bad it was. He had known that all was not well, for he could see the damage to his leg and his arm, but what he saw of his face made his stomach turn.

What was to become of him? When the Brits came back to drive Hitler and his troops out of France and back to Germany, and he was sure they would, would he go home or would he stay here with Michelle?

Chapter 13

Christmas 1942 was a quiet affair for people in the village. Turkeys were virtually unobtainable and as for a round of beef, well, forget it and dream on. But there were alternatives and Dorrie provided a brace of pheasants for Christmas dinner at the Jolliffes. No, she wouldn't tell them how and where she got them. Puddings and cakes fell short when it came to dried fruit even though that commodity had been hoarded specifically for them. As for sugar icing that was nothing but a fantasy.

Paper decorations that had been carefully hoarded were taken out of boxes and supplemented with the traditional holly and ivy, hung and pinned and looped round front rooms. Children made paper chains by painting and gluing strips of paper then sticking them together. Christmas trees were put up and decorated, but presents were few and far between and most of those were home-made.

But now Christmas and New Year were over and it was spring. Lucas at seventeen months was growing fast. He was a happy baby and a joy to his mother. Many were the cuddles they enjoyed, and when she tickled him his chuckles made her laugh.

They were in the garden and Dorrie had parked Luc, in his pram, in a sheltered spot while she started to dig the garden and prepare it, ready to sow seeds. She had been working steadily and was about ready for a break when she heard someone call her name. She looked up and there was Rosie, the customer she was always happy to see come into the shop, and who had become a friend. Rosie carried her two year old daughter balanced on her hip while she held her four year old son by the hand.

'How nice of you to come and visit,' she said.

'I should have come long before this,' said Rosie. 'I would have if I'd known that this was where you hid yourself. What an isolated spot. Don't you get lonely here on your own?'

'But I'm not on my own, am I?' said Dorrie. 'I've got Luc now and while I'm at home Moss never leaves my side.'

'Yes, but I don't suppose Luc is capable of intelligent conversation yet, is he? And anything you say to the dog has got to be one sided.'

'No, Luc doesn't talk much, but he's wonderful company.' Dorrie stuck the fork she was using in the ground and left it. 'I was just thinking about having a break so how about we have a cup of tea and you can tell me what I've done to deserve this visit.'

Rosie put her little one down and taking her two toddlers by the hand followed Dorrie as she pushed the pram into the house. 'I need someone to come to the dances with me,' she said. 'Lottie Steven's gone and joined up now and I really don't like to go alone. A girl on her own is a sitting duck as far as some of the men are concerned. Now that Luc's old enough to be left with my mum, who looks after my lot, why don't you come with me?'

Dorrie busied herself with making tea. She had tried the excuse of not being able to dance and that of having nothing to wear when Rosie had asked her before. There was no alternative now but to use them again.

'Dancing's not hard and I can teach you,' said Rosie. 'And are you sure you haven't got a best frock tucked away somewhere?'

'I never needed one because we didn't go anywhere,' said Dorrie. She thought about the dresses she had found in the bottom of the blanket box. But they were her mother's and probably wouldn't fit her. 'The only ones I've got are one's that I found in my mum's things, but I don't think they'll do.'

'Why not? Let me have a look at them.'

Hoping Rosie would say they were no use, Dorrie fetched the dresses. 'Sorry mum, I hope you don't mind,' she whispered as she carried them down the stairs.

'My gosh,' said an open mouthed Rosie. 'These are classy. You won't get stuff like that these days. Where did you get them?'

'They won't fit,' said Dorrie. 'They're too long.'

'We'll see about that. Try them on.' When Dorrie hesitated she said, 'It's all right, I won't look if you're shy.'

Dorrie had never undressed in front of anyone but her mother so she was glad when Rosie turned her head away. When she put the first dress on she was amazed at the sensuous feel of the material on her skin. But it was too loose and too long.

'I did tell you they wouldn't fit,' she said.

'That's okay.' Rosie grinned. 'Scissors and a needle and thread can soon put that right. I can do that for you and when I've made you look like a princess you'll come to the dance, won't you?'

'I suppose I could give it a try.'

'Right, take it off and try the other one and we'll see which looks best.'

There was not much to choose between them but Dorrie favoured the plainest. Beads and embroidery were party wear and it wasn't a party she was going to.

'There's just one other thing,' said Rosie. 'Did the undertaker give you your mother's wedding ring?' Dorrie nodded. 'Good, wear it then. It does help to keep the wolves at bay.'

'Whatever do you mean?'

Rosie looked at Dorrie. 'My dear girl, did your mother teach you nothing? Some men won't take no for an answer but if they think you're married it does put them off.'

'When you say things like that, Rosie, I wonder if it's safe for either of us to go.'

'Getting cold feet are you?'

'Well . . .' Dorrie hung her head. 'I've never been to a dance. I don't want to be thought of as a loose woman.'

Rosie laid Dorrie's dresses on the table and stood up. She put her arm round her friend. 'I'm a married woman, Dorrie,' she said. 'My man is out there on the high seas. As long as the German's don't sink the ship he's on he'll come home to me. If I sat at home and worried about him I'd go quietly mad. So I go out and dance and that's all I do. I belong to my Tom and no one else. I'm not going to lead you into trouble so smile and say you'll come with me.'

How could she refuse when Rosie put it like that? 'All right,' said Dorrie.

Rosie's little ones had gone outside to play, she gathered them up put the two year old in a pushchair, took the hand of the other and, with the two dresses in a bag, set off for home. 'I'll let you know when I'm ready for you to come and try them on,' she said.

With Luc in her arms Dorrie watched her go. She hoped her mother would approve of her dresses being cut and reshaped and wondered if Isobel had danced the night away when she had worn them. How little she knew about her or about her life before she met Reuben. Would she ever know or would that be forever a closed book?

Rosie lost no time in getting out scissors, needle and thread, and only a few days after she had offered to remodel Dorrie's dress she was in the shop telling her to come for a fitting.

'I envy you,' she said. 'You couldn't buy stuff like the material your dresses are made of these days. They must have cost a fortune when they were new. Where did you say you got them?'

'They were in the bottom of my mother's blanket box, but that doesn't mean to say they were hers so I don't know where they came from.'

'Well that doesn't matter,' said Rosie. 'Come along to my place when you shut shop. It will save you having to make a special journey.'

Not used to undressing in front of strangers, Dorrie shyly took off her everyday clothes and let Rosie slip the first of the altered dresses over her head. Rosie um'd and ah'd then said, 'Let's try the other one.'

The second dress was plainer than the first and Dorrie liked it better. Rosie, arms akimbo, stood and stared at her.

'The dress is beautiful' she said, 'but your shoes are awful. You cannot wear them. Are they all you've got?'

Dorrie looked down at her feet. 'Well, except for boots, yes. I've never needed anything else.'

'Did you *never* go anywhere, Dorrie? Did you *never* need a good pair of shoes? What size do you take?'

'Five I think.'

'Same as me. I'll lend you a pair.'

When Dorrie was suitably shod Rosie said, 'You look totally different now. In fact, you look quite the lady. Give us a twirl.' Dorrie obliged and Rosie clapped. 'Why did your mum and dad hide you up at Leanacres all this time? No, don't answer that. I guess they were stay at homes and of course if they didn't go out, neither could you.'

'There was always so much to do,' said Dorrie

'Well, now you can make up for lost time. Be here for six o'clock on Saturday.'

Chapter 14

'Now remember,' said Rosie as she and Dorrie walked arm in arm towards the village hall and the dance, 'when you are asked what your name is and where you live, and some man surely will ask, only tell him your first name, *never* anything else. Okay?'

'Okay,' said Dorrie.

'And if he asks you to go outside with him for some fresh air because it's too hot in the hall say no. It isn't the fresh air he wants, it's a chance to get fresh with you and you *don't* want that.'

'Don't worry, Rosie, I promise I'll behave myself.'

All the little doubts that had assailed Dorrie regarding the wisdom of agreeing to go to the dance surfaced again at Rosie's words. From what her friend was saying the men who would be there were nothing more than predatory animals. What was she letting herself in for? Why had she agreed? She had never learned how to dance, was well aware that she didn't know how to handle a conversation with a stranger, and now she was about to be pitched into a room full of them. She wanted to stop right there, turn around and go home, but almost as though she was aware of Dorrie's thoughts Rosie held tight to her arm. As they neared the village hall the beat of a drum and the sound of music carried to them.

A group of men in uniform were milling round the door of the hall.

'They're yanks,' said Rosie.

'Why are they all outside?'

'They always do that. I think they want to get first look at the girls who are going in. Our boys don't like them. They say they're pinching all their girlfriends. Not surprising really, the yanks get paid a lot more that our lot do. Come on, grin and follow me.'

The men parted to make way for Rosie and Dorrie to go through. 'Hi Rosie,' said one. 'Who's your friend?'

'Hi,' said Rosie as she dragged Dorrie along with her. 'You'll find out.'

'I sure will.'

'Who was that?' asked Dorrie as they hung their coats in the cloakroom.

'I don't know, just one of the blokes. Let's go and get a seat.'

They sat close to the stage on which the band, a man on drums and another with an accordion on his knee, a pianist and a fiddle player, were taking a rest. Local girls already in the room stood about in knots talking and giggling with the Americans. More were coming in and the hall was filling up. The sound of laughter and excited voices sent the noise level soaring. There was a mutter of words among the band as they agreed what they were going to play, then the fiddle player stood up grabbed the microphone and said, 'Take your partners for the quickstep, please.' The band struck up and straight away couples were on the floor.

Rosie was up and on her feet. 'Come on Dorrie, let's have a go?' she said.

'I'd rather watch for a while,' said Dorrie.

'Okay,' said Rosie. She turned as a hand touch her arm and a voice said, 'Dance with me, ma'am?'

'Sure will,' she said.

Dorrie watched her go then settled down to watch the feet of the dancers. But they went too fast. Quick step was certainly the right name for the dance - feet seemed to be flying in all directions. I'll never learn that she thought so gave up and turned to watch and listen to the band.

'Would you dance with me, Ma'am?'

Dorrie looked up at the tall man who stood and smiled at her. 'I'm sorry but I can't, I don't know how,' she said.

'Then may I sit with you a while?'

'If you like.'

He sat down beside her. 'Have you never learned to dance?' he asked.

'No. And if I'd known it was as fast and as furious as this I don't think I'd have agreed to come tonight.'

'It's not always like this, but the guy's love to jitterbug.'

'Is that what you call it?'

'Yea, that's it. My name's John,' said the man. 'I'm from Nebraska. What can I call you?'

'Oh. I'm Dorrie.' Where on earth was Nebraska?

'So why are you at a dance if you don't know how?' asked John.

'My friend wanted me to come with her. She said she'd teach me.'

'But she's away with someone else.'

'That's all right. I was happy for her to go.'

'You're kind.' The man from Nebraska smiled at her and Dorrie liked it. In fact she liked the look of him and found talking to him easy. Why had she been so worried about it?

'Hi,' said Rosie when the music stopped and the dancers dispersed to their chosen corners of the room. 'Who's this then?'

'My name's John Houseman, ma'am. I was talking to your friend. I thought she looked lonely.'

'Well, I'm here now.'

But not for long, as the band struck up again Rosie was whirled away.

'Don't you want to find a partner and go and dance?' asked Dorrie. 'You don't have to stay here with me you know.'

'I'd rather just sit and talk. Tell me about England. It's a cosy little country, I love it. I see you're wearing a wedding band. Where is your husband?'

She would have to lie; there was nothing else for it. Rosie had told her not to give anything away so Dorrie said, 'He's in the army. I don't know quite where he is at the moment.' Well, that was true. 'And I've never heard England called cosy before.'

John laughed. 'Compared to the open spaces back home it's cute.'

'And what about you? Do you like being in the army?'

'I guess I'd rather be at home. But that man from Germany has to be stopped. You surely don't have any children, do you?'

'I'm afraid I do. I have a little boy, Luc.'

'And you have family to help you out.'

'No. My parents are both dead.' Oh, too much information. 'But I have good friends. They're a great help and I couldn't manage without them. That's the beauty of living in a village.'

It was easy to talk to John, and what could be wrong with bending the truth a little? Who was going to know? Dorrie relaxed and enjoyed his company. He was different, not like Garnet who was bursting with energy and full of fun. This man tended towards seriousness, though when he smiled it was warm and enveloping and Dorrie found herself thinking that she would very much like to see him again, would like to get to know him. So they talked and the evening slipped away.

'Please take your partners for the last waltz,' announced the fiddle player.

'Is it that time already?' said Dorrie.

'Yes,' said John. 'And you're going to do this with me.' He stood up and taking Dorrie by the hand, pulled her up off her chair.

'But I can't,' said Dorrie as his arm went round her.

'Yes, you can,' he said.

His hand in the middle of her back, he pulled her close and held her tight. She looked up at him. He smiled and Dorrie, looking at his mouth, wondered what it would be like if he kissed her.

'Put your hand on my arm,' said John as he held her other. 'Follow my steps, slow and easy.'

Slow and easy it was. But he was a stranger and she was in an intimate embrace with him. She could feel the warmth of him, could feel the smoothness of his uniform when she lowered her head and her cheek brushed against it. He held her close but pulled her even closer. His breath was warm on her ear and the side of her neck. It made her heart beat faster.

Oblivious to everyone around her, Dorrie gave herself up to the lilt of the music and the thrill of being held in the arms of the man who guided her so effortlessly round the room. At last it was over and the band was playing *God Save the King*.

Rosie was there. 'Come on, let's get our coats and get home,' she said and dragged Dorrie away.

'I didn't say goodnight to him,' protested Dorrie when they were in the cloakroom. 'You didn't give me time.'

'What about it?' Rosie gave Dorrie a little punch with a closed fist. 'Hey, you didn't promise him anything, did you?'

'No, of course I didn't. But he was nice.'

'Yea, they all are to start with. Grow up, Dorrie.'

Chapter 15

'Well, how did you enjoy the dance?' asked Susan.

'It was very crowded and extremely noisy,' said Dorrie. 'There were a lot of

American soldiers there. They looked very smart.'

'And did Rosie teach you to dance?'

'She might have done if she'd had time. But I don't know if I want to learn. I don't think I want to be thrown about the way some of the girls were.'

'What do you mean?'

'They call it the jitterbug. Rosie was good at it. She's very popular and I think she danced every dance.'

'And what did you do then?'

Kneeling on the floor behind the counter, Dorrie was stacking the shelves under it with tins of baked beans and sardines.

'I sat and watched and then one of the Americans came and asked me to dance. When I said I couldn't he sat down and talked to me. I thought he was very nice. And then he made me do the last waltz with him. I liked it.'

'Tell me that was all and that you're not going to see him again.'

'Of course I'm not going to see him, how could I?' said Dorrie.

'Oh dear, oh dear,' said Susan. 'Here comes trouble. Stay where you are, Dorrie, and don't get up on any account.'

'Why?'

'Ssssh. Hello Bill,' said Susan as a young man came into the shop. 'We don't see you this way very often. What can I do for you?'

'Ounce of Golden Virginia, Mrs Jolliffe, if you don't mind.'

'Still smoking then. Will that be all?'

'Better have some Rizla's, the green ones.'

Susan put the tobacco and cigarette papers on the counter and held out her hand for payment.

'I hear you've got a pretty new assistant, Mrs Jolliffe. Where is she then?'

'She's not here today,' said Susan as she took Bill Dewey's money then handed him his change.

'Aw that's a shame,' said Bill. 'I was looking forward to seeing her.'

'And why would you want to do that? Aren't you and Burt Mullin's daughter about to get wed?'

'Huh. That's been called off. Her mother reckons I'm not good enough.'

And she's right thought Susan. If I had a daughter I wouldn't let you within a half mile of her. 'I expect you'll find someone else,' she said. But it won't be Dorrie. 'Goodbye Bill.'

'I'll see you again then,' said the young man as he left the shop.

Susan waited until Bill Dewey was on his way down the road before she said, 'You can come up now, Dorrie.'

Dorrie stood up and stretched her legs. 'Who was that?'

'That was someone you don't want to know and if you ever see him coming run a mile. He has one illegitimate child that we know about, there are probably others. He's been walking out with the daughter of the farmer he works for, but you heard what he said, that's off so he's looking for someone else and he's got his sights on you.'

'Thanks for warning me, Susan, but I can look after myself.'

'Well, I'm not too sure about that. You'd better be careful. Now then, you were telling me about the American.'

'Yes, he was nice, but I don't know anything about him except his name and where he comes from, and I didn't tell him anything about me. Rosie said I shouldn't.'

'I'm glad to hear it. Now, how would you like a day out? I'm going to shut the shop all day on Wednesday. I want to go and see my sister. She's already lost one of her sons and she's been having a hard time. The people she works for haven't been able to replace any of the indoor staff that left to join up and now she has to do the work of two. It's telling on her and I thought that a visit might cheer her up. I wondered if you'd like to come with me.'

'Is it very far?'

'We'll have to go by bus. It's an hour's journey. I could do with your company. You never go anywhere so it would be a day out for you and I think you'd enjoy it. You could leave Luc with Rosie.'

'I think I would like that, Mrs Jolliffe.'

*

In all her short life Dorrie had never been more than a few miles from her home at Leanacres; there had been no need. A journey on a bus had never been more than the three short miles into the town. The bus she and Susan were on now was crowded and they were lucky to be able to sit together. As it wended its way through villages and country lanes passengers were dropped and others picked up. Dorrie, in her seat by the window, was fascinated with the passing scene. She marvelled at what she saw, cattle and sheep in fields that were lush and green, unlike the hungry acres at her home. She was dazzled by the glint of the sun on a river, delighted to see apple orchards coming into bloom and flowers in the front gardens of cottages.

'It's all so pretty, isn't it?' she said to Susan. 'I'm glad you asked me to come.'

'It'll be better still in summer,' said Susan. 'Pick up your bag; this is our stop, it's time to get off.'

When they were standing on the side of the road watching the bus pull away she said, 'We have to walk now, but not far.'

Not far was a short distance along the road, through an impressive gateway and then along a tree lined drive. As the house came into view Dorrie stopped and stared.

'Oh my goodness, you didn't tell me that your sister lived in a great big house like this.'

Susan laughed. 'Well, she does, but it's not hers. She's cook for Lord Melchett, been here for years.'

When the drive forked into two and one veered away from the front of the house Susan said, 'We have to go this way. It's the back door for servants.'

It may have been the back door, but it was big, made of wood and fitted with a black iron knocker. When she compared it to her own door, a door that didn't fit particularly well, Dorrie thought that it was very grand. Susan lifted the knocker and banged it down a couple of times.

The woman who opened the door wore a large white apron, her hair pinned under a cap. A few strands had escaped. At the sight of Susan she burst into tears.

'Now, now, Mabel, don't take on so,' said Susan. 'I'm here and look I've brought a drop of milk for our tea not to make you short.'

Mabel took a handkerchief from her pocket and dried her eyes. 'Short, huh. We don't go short of anything here. Come on in.'

'So what's upset you now?' asked Susan.

'I am *so* tired,' said Mabel. 'The kitchen maid's gone now so I have to get up at six to light the fire in the range and then it's all go with only about an hour's rest in the afternoon. I never get finished before nine at night and then all I do is drop into bed.'

They sat in the servant's hall, a small room with a table and chairs and easy chairs each side of a fireplace. Mabel Carter made them tea and added a plate of scones with jam and cream. Dorrie sat at the table and listened as the sisters talked.

'I don't know how much longer I can go on here,' said Mabel. 'We've only got a housemaid and a parlour maid, it's not enough, and as for a kitchen maid, well I'd like to see one, they're like gold dust. I have to clean as well as cook. I only asked you to come today because I knew Georgina and Jocelin were going to be away and his Lordship said he was going out to lunch.'

'But what would you do if you were to leave? Where would you go?'

'I don't know. Perhaps I could get another job, something lighter.'

'Excuse me,' said Dorrie. 'I want to go to the bathroom, where is it?'

'Oh dear, I'm sorry, we're forgetting you aren't we. It's just along the corridor,' said Mabel. 'You can't miss it.'

Just along the corridor, thought Dorrie as she walked along a flagstone passageway. She pushed open a door at the end and stepped, not into a bathroom but into a carpeted hall. It was warm. It was silent. It was in total contrast to the room she had just left. I don't think this is right she thought. I shouldn't be here, but the family are all out or should be if Mabel Carter's right so it won't matter. She took a step forward.

The hall she was in was vast. Richly coloured carpets lay on a polished wooden floor. Small occasional tables held vases of flowers. The ceiling was high. The walls were panelled and on them hung ornately framed oil paintings, mostly portraits.

The first one Dorrie looked at was of a florid faced man in riding clothes, a dog at his side. She cringed mentally as he appeared to look down his haughty nose at her. She moved on to the next. This was of a young woman whose hair was looped up and decked with a string of pearls. She wore a low cut evening gown, more pearls round her neck.

There were rings on her fingers and one was identical to one of those she had found in her mother's trinket box. Dorrie held her breath as she stared at the face that was as familiar to her as her own.

It wasn't a word. It wasn't even a whisper. It came on her outgoing breath, 'Mama.'

'She's beautiful, isn't she?'

Dorrie spun round. A tall man stood smiling at her, a smile that dropped abruptly when he saw her face. 'Isobel,' he said. 'No it can't be. Who are you, what are you doing here?'

'I'm so sorry,' said Dorrie. 'I wanted to go to the bathroom and I've come the wrong way.' She turned to go.

'No, wait,' said the man. 'You appeared to be fascinated by that portrait. Do you know who it is?'

'I thought I did, but it can't be. I thought it was my mother.'

The man stood and stared at her. 'They say everyone has a double, don't they? What did you say you were doing here?'

'Mrs Jolliffe brought me with her to see Mrs Carter, her sister. I'm trespassing. I'm sorry. I'll go now.'

He didn't ask her to stay and Dorrie hurried back to the servant's hall. 'I went the wrong way,' she said. 'Can you tell me again how to find a toilet?'

Successful this time Dorrie was glad when at last Susan said they'd better get a move on or they'd miss the bus. Susan wanted to talk as they journeyed home but Dorrie was withdrawn and quiet. There was too much to think about.

'What's the matter with you?' asked Susan. 'You were full of life on the way up and now you've changed completely. Didn't you like Apsley Hall?'

'It was beautiful, but far too big for a family.'

'My dear, they're moneyed people, not like us. They don't have to scratch for a living. Did it affect you that much then? Do you want to tell me about it?'

'No, Mrs Jolliffe, I don't. Perhaps I will one day.'

Chapter 16

What an unequal place the world was thought Dorrie. Why could people like Lord Melchett live in luxury while others were scraping the bottom of the barrel? And why was her mother's portrait hanging in his house? Was it there because he collected paintings? Some people did. Or was his family the one who had banished Isobel from their midst because she had fallen in love with the stable boy? If that was the case then the man she had been talking to might be her uncle. And if he was why hadn't he told her? But no, he wouldn't do that, would he? She was a stranger to him, he to her, and hadn't he said that everyone had a double and that was why he thought that she looked like the girl in the painting? Forget it, Dorrie, she told herself.

It was June; peas were ready to pick and runner beans beginning to flower. She had been working in the garden all morning, later she would pull carrots ready to take to the shop tomorrow. She had been glad when Susan said she would take the surplus vegetables to sell. The extra money they brought in was very welcome, but even so her purse was rarely full to bursting.

Luc, asleep in the pram which Dorrie had put in the shade, began to stir. She bent over him and drank in the wonder of him. He opened his eyes and looked at her, smiled, waved his chubby arms then kicked off the blanket that covered him. He chuckled and gurgled and Moss, hearing him put her feet on the side of the pram and tail waving madly looked in at him. How Dorrie wished that Garnet could be here to see them. Would he ever come back to her?

'Hi Dorrie.' It was Rosie with her toddlers in tow. 'I see you're doing a bit of baby worship. They're so beautiful when they're that age, aren't they?'

'This one certainly is. What can I do for you?'

'Oh, well, it's a nice day so I just thought I'd get the kids out of doors and come and see what you are doing. I have a message for you.'

'Oh, who from?'

'Would the name John ring any bells?'

'You mean the man from Nebraska, don't you? What does he want?'

'He wants to see you again.'

Dorrie allowed herself a little smile of pleasure. It was nice to think that someone liked her enough to want to see more of her. She'd very much like to see him again, but as much as she did she couldn't allow it. He had been constantly in her thoughts and she had even been tempted to think that if it hadn't been for Garnet she could easily fall in love with him.

'Well he can want on,' she said. 'He was very nice and I did like him, but I don't think I ought to see him.'

'I thought you might say that and I did tell him. I suppose I shall just have to say it again. But Dorrie, there's no reason why you shouldn't see him, is there? I mean, you aren't promised to Garnet are you?'

There was a pause before Dorrie replied. 'Not in so many words. But I did promise to wait.'

'Well then,' said Rosie. 'There's no reason why you can't see anyone you like, not only that, but nobody knows what's happened to Garnet and you might never see him again.'

'I know, but his mum swears that he will come home and I do want him to. After all, Lucas is his son.'

'But that doesn't mean you have to live like a hermit until he does. You're young; you shouldn't deny yourself the chance to have some fun.'

Dorrie lifted a now fully awake Luc from his pram. 'Mm,' she said. 'I think this one wants some dry pants. Let's go inside, it's too hot for the little ones to stay out here. And Rosie, if I happen to bump into John somewhere that's okay, but no way am I going to arrange to meet him anywhere, so let's not talk about it.'

In the house Dorrie put Luc into some dry clothes then, giving Rosie's children a box of bricks, set him down on the floor to play with them. 'I'm not going to make tea,' she said. 'But there's a pitcher of fresh water if you want a drink.'

'That would be nice,' said Rosie. 'Water from a spring tastes far better than the stuff from the tap.' Then as Dorrie sat down opposite her, 'How did you like your trip with Mrs Jolliffe the other day?'

'It was nice to be able to see other places and houses and gardens and stuff.'

'And what about the big house, what did you think of that?'

'Well,' Dorrie hesitated, leaned back in her chair. Should she tell Rosie what happened? 'It looked all right.'

'Only all right? I thought it would be as big as Buckingham Palace if what Susan says is true.'

'It is big, but I don't think it's that big. We were there to see Susan's sister and not the people who own the place. The kitchen she works in would contain my house with room to spare. It was huge. And then there was a scullery as well and Mrs Carter has to keep all that clean as well as cooking the meals. It's nothing more than slavery. No wonder she was upset. We had a cup of tea and something to eat and then I had to sit and wait while Mrs Jolliffe and her sister talked.'

'Weren't you bored?'

'Yes, I was a bit, but then I wanted to go to the bathroom and I went the wrong way and got into the front of the house. I didn't think there was anyone there. Susan's sister said they were all out, but they weren't and I got caught.'

Rosie grinned and leaned forward on her chair. 'So what happened?' A squabble over bricks took her attention away from her friend. 'Play nicely you two or I won't bring you here again,' she said. Quarrel settled she turned back to Dorrie. 'So go on, I'm dying to know.'

'At first I thought it was beautiful; there were carpets everywhere, thick and soft and when you walk on them there's no sound. There were big pots of flowers on little tables and paintings of people and horses hanging on the wall.'

'Go on, go on, that can't be all.'

Dorrie rubbed her hands together; she was agitated and unsure of how to go on. 'Listen Rosie . . . um . . . um . . . You must promise never to tell anyone about what I'm going to tell you. I'll never forgive you if you do, promise.'

'Cross my heart and hope to die,' said Rosie. 'What is it?'

'One of the paintings was a portrait of my mother.'

'*WHAT?*'

'I was looking at it and then there was a man behind me. I hadn't heard him coming because of the carpet. He said, "She's beautiful, isn't she?" He made me jump and when I turned round he gasped and he said,

76

"Isobel." That was my mother's name. And then he wanted to know who I was and why I was there.'

'Oh, my God, Dorrie, do you think . . . no . . . who was it? And why did they have a painting of your mum? It was your mum, wasn't it?'

'I'm sure it was. And this is the strange thing. When I was cleaning out Mum's bedroom I found a letter she'd written to me to find when she'd gone. She said her parents were moneyed people and when I thought about it, I wondered if it could be them. Why else would they have a painting of my mother?'

Shocked into disbelief, Rosie leaned forward and slapped her hands on the table. 'Oh my God, but that would explain the dresses wouldn't it?' she squeaked.

'I don't know,' Dorrie huffed. 'I don't want to think about it, but that's why you mustn't say anything. Okay?'

'Okay. But . . .'

'*No*, you promised.' Dorrie jumped up and shoved her chair back under the table. 'You're *not* to say a word. I shouldn't have told you so I'm not going to talk about it anymore.'

'Okay, okay, keep your hair on,' said Rosie. 'I won't say anything.'

'Mind you don't then. I've got to get on now, I've got to fetch water for the copper, it's washing day tomorrow.'

'And it's time I was getting home with these two. Come on, you little terrors. Give Lucas back his bricks. I'll tell John what you said when I see him then. Bye.'

*

June became July and the trees in the wood began to look tired, the freshness of their green became dull and the rough herbage of the common died away to beige. The green peas were over, runner beans were in full spate, and it was time to dig the early potatoes. Summer was bowing out and autumn was on the horizon. It was time to gather kindling for her winter fires so Dorrie made a sling to carry Luc on her back while she went to the woods to gather it.

She was in the garden picking a basket of runner beans to take to the shop when she heard the sound of a car coming up the track. Very few visitors came to Leanacres and none ever in a car. She stopped what she was doing and, carrying Luc, went to see who it was.

The car was new, clean and brightly polished. It shone in the sunlight. In the driver's seat was a man who wore a peaked cap. Who round here could afford a chauffeur? The car stopped by Dorrie's door. The chauffeur got out and opened the rear passenger door. Highly polished shoes were the first to appear, then the legs of a tailored suit, and finally the figure of Lord Melchett. He stood and looked at Dorrie.

'So this is where you live,' he said.

Chapter 17

Why was he here? Dorrie was not inclined to welcome him. 'What do you want?'

'Can we go inside? I wish to speak with you.' Lord Melchett held out a hand to indicate that she should precede him into the house. She wanted to refuse but at the same time wanted to hear what he had to say so what else could she do? She led the way. In her living room she put Lucas in his pram then turned to look at her visitor.

'Why are you here? What can you possibly want with me?'

'When I saw you at Apsley Hall you were the embodiment of my sister, Isobel. I believe that your mother could be her. I loved her very much and when my parents banished and disowned her I thought I would never see her again.'

'And if she *was* your sister you are not going to now. She died.'

'Ah, I am too late. I should have been looking for her before this. But although you look like her I need proof before I can claim you as my niece. What is your father's name?'

'My father is also dead, but he was known as Reuben Bartlett.'

'Reuben Bartlett, yes that was the name of the stable boy. Do you have your parents' marriage certificate?'

'No. At least if there is one I haven't found it.'

'No matter, it is possible to get a copy. You are so like your mother that there cannot be any doubt that you are my niece, but I will instruct my solicitor to look further into the matter. I'm sure that it will be nothing but a formality though.' Alasdair, Lord Melchett, smiled. 'I am so happy to have found you. I want to make up for all the wrong done to your mother. Now that I see how and where you live I would like to take you away from it. You should not be living like this. I can offer you and your child a home with me at Apsley Hall. It is your right.'

In her letter her mother had said that her family were moneyed people, but also that she didn't want her daughter to look for them. There must be a reason for that. Dorrie had been standing, now she pulled out a chair and sat down.

'No, you're wrong,' she said. 'You are nothing to me.'

'But my dear, when you looked at your mother's portrait did you not wonder why

it hung there? Did it not occur to you that she belonged in that house?'

'The picture may have belonged, but that does not mean that my mother did. You could have bought the portrait to add to your collection. That's what people do; invest in paintings, don't they?'

'Yes, you're right, they do. But I remember that portrait being painted. Isobel was so patient that if the artist asked she would sit for him for hours. The longer I look at you the more convinced I am that Isobel, your mother, was my sister. I did not agree with the harsh treatment my parents gave her. I thought that given time she would tire

of and leave your father. She was only sixteen. There were many young men who were eminently more suitable that she could have had, but she was headstrong and the more she was told to give your father up the more she was determined not to.'

Lord Melchett smiled as he reminisced. 'Yes, she was a very determined young lady. But I am an old man now and before it's too late I would like to redress the balance.'

What balance? Again Dorrie thought of how Isobel had written in that letter that she didn't want Dorrie to try to find the family she had come from.

'You do not live here alone, do you?' asked Lord Melchett. 'Where is your husband?'

Thank you, Rosie, for telling me to wear mama's ring. 'He's in the army.'

'Then how do you manage?'

It was Dorrie's turn to smile. This man, an aristocrat who was waited on hand and foot, would have no idea what sort of life she led. But it seemed he wanted to so she told him how she cared for the garden. How she got sweet water from a spring. How she took buckets down to the stream to fetch water to fill the copper. How she built a fire under it to heat the water with which to wash her clothes and how she gathered wood for that fire and the one in her living room over which she would boil a kettle or cook her dinner.

'It was the way my mother and father always did it and I see no reason to alter it. I love living here and I will stay and look after house and land until the day I die.'

'My God, is that the way my sister lived? She was not brought up to do menial work. Why did she not come back to us? If she had begged forgiveness surely she would have been taken back. Oh, poor Isobel. She could not have known what her life was going to be. I'm sure she must have hated it. Why on earth did she stay?'

'My mother and father were devoted to one another, neither wanted things to change. I am sure she never had a moment's doubt about her decision to live here. If she had wanted to leave my father would not have stopped her. All he wanted was her happiness and they were happy - really happy.'

'But you don't have to struggle to make a living. I would like you and your little boy to come and live with me and my family. I can give you so much. I can pay for your son's education. I can give you the sort of life you deserve. Please humour me and agree. It would help disperse some of the guilt I feel at not having done more for Isobel. I should not have delayed looking for her.'

'But I don't want to live with you. I'm quite happy where I am.'

'You don't know what you're saying.'

Dorrie stood up, turned, and gripped the back of her chair. 'I know exactly what I'm saying. My mother and father had nowhere to go until they found this house. It had been abandoned. They moved in and made it a home. They worked to win land from the gorse and scrub that covered it. They dug a garden. They taught me what I had to do to survive. I would be letting them down if I left it so I will not desert Leanacres. Not even for you and the life you offer.'

Alasdair Carteret studied the young woman who defied him. She was truly Isobel's daughter. Isobel had defied her parents and paid a heavy price for it. Had she ever regretted her decision to abandon money and position for this lowly dwelling and hardship as the wife of a labourer? That was something he would never know. But would her daughter regret turning down his offer? He would keep it open and hope that she would change her mind.

'I am not going to accept your refusal,' he said. 'I would like you to give it some thought. And whether you change your mind or not I shall come to visit you again. Now I must go.'

He stood up. Dorrie saw him out and watched as his chauffer opened a door for him, waited while he climbed in then drove him away. There was no doubt they had been seen in the village; enquiries as to where she lived had probably been made at the shop, and now the place would be ripe with gossip. How was she going to cope with the battery of questions the customers would throw at her?

Chapter 18

Tousle headed and bleary eyed, Dorrie pulled herself up from her bed. She had spent a troubled and sleepless night. The visit of Lord Melchett had upset her. Endless questions had presented themselves, questions that had no answers. Could it be possible that his family was the one her mother belonged to? If so that might explain the dresses, the satin shoes and the jewellery. But why had her mother said that she would not like Dorrie to try to find out who her parents were? Was there some awful family secret?

'Mama, mama.' Luc was rattling the side of his cot.

'All right, darlin'. Mummy's coming.'

Dorrie put on her clothes, wrapped her son in a shawl and carried him down the stairs. There she put him into his pram while she lit the fire.

If she took up the offer to live at Apsley Hall, she would not have to boil a kettle in order to have hot water. She would be able to turn on a tap and there would be as much as she wanted. She wouldn't have to gather wood to make the fire, wouldn't have to light it and wait for the kettle to boil. How lovely that would be.

She filled a glass with water from the pitcher, offered some to Luc then had a drink herself. When they were washed, dressed and fed, Dorrie took Luc in his pram to the garden where she pulled a large bunch of carrots. She put them along with a bag of potatoes into the well in the bottom of the pram. Susan had unearthed it from an outbuilding at the back of the shop and given it to her. It was not a very pretty carriage but with a clean and a polish its lack of good looks was more than compensated for by its usefulness. It was one more thing that customers who were kind and understanding had presented to her when it had become obvious she was going to have a baby. Rosie had given her outgrown baby clothes and someone else a cot.

At the shop a beaming Susan Jolliffe met her. 'Why did his Lordship . . .?'

Dorrie held up her hand. 'Don't ask,' she said.

'Oh but . . .'

'I'm not going to tell you.'

'Well, you'd better hide then. I think all the village knows he was looking for you and we all want to know why. There is no way you can keep it a secret so you might as well tell us.'

She'd known this was going to happen. Villages were communities where there were no secrets. Families were interrelated and everyone knew everyone else's business. She would have a hard job to keep the reason for Lord Melchett's visit private.

Luc had settled down for his morning nap so Dorrie parked the pram out of doors in the shade at the side of the shop. She was ready to get on with some work, but her problem was not going to go away and her attention was not on it. It would have to wait though, a customer was coming into the shop and she hadn't seen him in time to hide. Bill Dewey grinned at her and took a step or two towards her.

'She's just as lovely as they said she was. I think my ship's come in,' he said.

'Did you want something?' said Dorrie. Oh, that was the wrong thing to say.

'Yes, oh yes. Just one little thing would make me a most happy man. Give us a kiss and come to the pictures with me. I've got the loan of a car. I can take you in style.'

'I don't want to go to the pictures.'

He was leaning on the counter now. 'Well, we can do something else. What would you like? Your wish is my command. I'll do anything you say.'

Dorrie stepped back out of arm's reach. 'Nothing . . . I . . . um. I don't want to go anywhere with you. Go away, just go away.'

'Oh, so you're going to act hoity-toity are you?' Bill Dewey stood up, put his hands flat on the counter then leaned towards her. 'I heard all about his Lordship coming to see you and you may think you're better than the rest of us in the village my lady, but you're not. I know where you live. I might just wander round and pay you a visit one day.'

'What's that you're saying?' Susan Jolliffe bustled in from the back room. 'Are you upsetting my assistant, Bill?'

'Not at all, Mrs J. I asked her out on a date and she turned me down. I'd have done anything she asked. Now I'm devastated.'

'You leave her alone. If she doesn't want to go out with you then that's that.'

'But I'm not going to give up. I quite fancy her.'

'I'm not going to tell you again, Bill. She's not for you.'

Bill Dewey laughed and stood arms akimbo. 'You might be a game old girl Mrs J, but not you or anyone else is going to stop me when I want something.'

'Game old girl indeed,' shouted Susan, 'get out of my shop before I wrap this brush round your ears.'

'But I came in for . . .'

'I don't care what you came in for. Go and get it somewhere else.'

'Oh, all right.' Bill Dewey opened the shop door then turned and pointed a finger at Dorrie, 'But you haven't seen the last of me, my beauty. I'll be back.' He slammed the door and was gone.

'Oh my golly, Susan, what am I going to do?'

'Keep your eyes and ears open and kick him where it hurts if he ever comes near you. I don't know what else. Drink your coffee.'

'I know I said I wasn't going to tell you, but I need to talk to you,' said Dorrie. 'In fact, I could do with your advice. But it will have to wait until dinner time.'

'Is this about your rich visitor?'

'Yes. I don't want anyone else to know so I'd like you to help me fend off the nosy parkers. You will, won't you?'

'Of course I will.'

It seemed that everyone in the village was in need of a few carrots, their butter ration, their portion of cheese or a few potatoes that morning and Susan and Dorrie were kept busy. Susan was more than capable of putting down blatant suppositions as to why a titled gentleman came to call on a person no better than themselves. She had had long practice, for the village shop was known to be the centre of gossip.

At last the morning's trade was over, the door shut behind the last customer, and the sign on it turned to CLOSED. Dorrie, with Luc in her arms, followed Susan into the kitchen.

'It's just a bit of cold meat and pickle today,' said Susan. 'I never got a chance to get out here and put a few potatoes on to boil, but there is a bit of apple pie left from yesterday.'

'That will do just fine,' said Dorrie.

'Now,' said Susan when they had finished eating and were drinking tea. 'What's bothering you? What do you want to tell me?'

'I hardly know where to begin,' said Dorrie. 'But when we went to see your sister and I wanted to go to the bathroom I ended up in the front of the house. I was in a room with lots of paintings and one was a portrait of my mother.'

Susan's mouth dropped open. '*Your mother?*' she gasped.

'Yes. And then a man, who I now know was Lord Melchett, was standing behind me. He was as shocked as you when I turned and looked at him. He said I was just like her. I always thought I was but seeing the picture proved it. And then he said he thought that my mother was his sister and that their parents had thrown her out because she'd fallen in love with my dad who was the stable boy. There's a lot more but that's why he came to see me. He wanted proof of who I was.'

'And were you able to give it to him?'

'Up to a point.'

'So what's the problem?'

'He wants me to give up Leanacres and go and live with him and his family at the Hall.'

'My God, Dorrie . . . oh . . . I don't know what to say.'

'He says he'll come again, says he'll pay for Luc's education, says that he can give me the sort of life that I deserve.'

'And what do you think of that?'

'He can whistle if he thinks I'm going to do what he wants.'

'But maybe you do belong there. When you came to work for me first I said to Reg that there was something about you that put you apart from the village girls. Something that said you ought to be dressed in silks and satins and not that old cotton dress you had on. I was right. There always was something of the lady about you. My goodness, here you are weighing up rations and selling carrots and onions to the folk in the village when you really belong in the big house. What are you going to do?'

'I don't know. That's just the trouble. I want to stay at Leanacres, but would I be depriving Lucas of something I'd never be able to give him? And what if Garnet does come home, what would I do then?'

Susan took a slurp of tea. 'There are other things for you to think about. We can cope with Lucas now but give it another year and he'll be more mobile and toddlers are notorious for getting into mischief. How are you going to cope with your work with him under your feet and come to that, am I going to be able to carry on employing you?'

'Oh, don't say that.'

'Well, I have to admit that it had crossed my mind. But now there's a door opening for you and a good offer to think about. It might be silly to turn it down flat. In any case you've got a lot to mull over. You have a good long think about it and when you're ready we'll talk again.'

Chapter 19

The Germans were jubilant. They had turfed the British off the soil of France and out of Europe. They were the master race. Men and women who were not Arian were subordinate to them, and arrogant and puffed with power they made the most of it. They plundered, stole and laid waste to what they couldn't take. When they came to Michelle's house they came in twos or threes, never alone. Garnet watched the strutting soldiers and was afraid for Michelle. Even though he and she had squirreled away what food they could they often went hungry after the soldiers had been. But they persevered. They dug and planted and grew vegetables. In the autumn they harvested their crops, buried potatoes in a pit some distance from the house, not all, for the Germans would hold them at gun point to show where they were if they suspected what they'd done. It was a game of cat and mouse and Garnet prayed for it to cease.

He had lived with Michelle for many, many months, had worked with her and Laurent, and though she looked after him and was kind to him he was no closer to knowing her than in the first few days he had been with her. Sometimes she left him home alone. "I have to go to work," she'd say and with a smile would leave him. And then, late at night, when he had been in the kitchen getting a glass of water, she, dressed in dark clothes, walked in. He hadn't asked her where she'd been, but guessed that she was a member of the resistance too, and that it would account for the times when somehow he knew that she was not in the house. He wished he could go with her, with them, so that he could do something to repay them for helping him.

There were other days when Michelle was at home, when the sun shone and they were happy. It was one of those when Michelle said, 'How old are you, Pierre? And when is your birthday?'

'I'm twenty four,' said Garnet. 'And my birthday was last week.'

'Ah! Non, non mon cher. Why did you not say? We must do something to celebrate. I will make for you the omelette au fromage and we will drink with it this wine that my friend gave me.'

'You don't have to do that, Michelle. There's nothing to celebrate.'

'Ah, but your maman would have made you a cake. I cannot do that so I will make the omelette and serve the wine.'

While Michelle beat eggs and grated cheese she said, 'I hear that England is getting ready to invade and drive the Hun out of France. I welcome the day. Would you pour the wine, Pierre?'

They sat to eat and, smiling and relaxed, drank wine and talked of what they would do when the country was free again.

'You will go home and marry your lover,' said Michelle. 'And you will live in a little house in the country with roses round the door. That's what the English do, don't they? You do have a lover, do you not?'

'I'd hardly call her that, a girlfriend maybe.'

'But she is pretty, eh?'

'Oh yes.' Garnet smiled as he visualised Dorrie. 'She has beautiful hair. It's soft and it curls and depending on the light it is sometimes red, mostly copper, but when the sun shines on it, it is spun gold, so beautiful.'

'And her eyes, what colour are her eyes?'

Garnet smiled, absorbed as he was in his visualisation of Dorrie. 'Sometimes they are green, sometimes nearly golden brown. I guess they'd be called hazel; yes that's it, hazel.'

'But you will marry her, won't you?'

The smile dropped from his face and Garnet said, 'How, with this face, can I even think to ask her? She should not have to look at it. She deserves better.'

'If she loves you enough no disfigurement will matter.'

'But it matters to me, Michelle. I don't like what I see when I look in a mirror. I don't want people to look at me as though I am a freak.'

'You are not a freak. But the injury to your face is something you will have to come to terms with. Are you going to stop living just because your face is not as you would want? There are many people who carry their injuries in public. If they can be accepted then so can you.' Michelle reached out and laid her hand gently on the scars on Garnet's face. She smiled. 'Give it time,' she said. 'Give it time.'

Suddenly the smile that was on her face faded. She sat up straight and turned her head to listen. 'What's that I hear?'

The sound of a motor coming to a stop, an engine switched off, the slam of a door then another and voices, German voices.

'Courage, mon ami,' said Michelle.

Jackboots clattered on the stone floor of the kitchen. 'Aha, Helmut, they have put out the wine to welcome us. You will find glasses for us, Mademoiselle?'

As Michelle took wine glasses from a cupboard one of the German soldiers slapped her bottom. Then he cupped it with his hand. 'Such a nice arsch.' He laughed.

The men sat down and helped themselves to Michelle's food. They laughed and joked as they drank the wine. Garnet had moved away from the table. He watched them, one in particular whose eyes constantly followed Michelle's every move. The wine bottle that was already opened was soon empty. The Germans were merry and asking for more. A second bottle was opened and the contents drunk.

The man Garnet had been watching turned to him. 'Is your frau?' he asked. Garnet shook his head. 'Ah, then is mine. Kommen sie hier meine damen,' he said to Michelle and beckoned her to him.

Nervously she approached. The man grabbed her and with one arm tight round her waist pulled her to him. His free hand he ran up her leg and under her skirt.

Garnet, fuming, saw Michelle turn towards him. She looked at him over the head of her abuser. Her eyes were dark and full of anger, her mouth closed in a tight little line. She gave a small shake of her head. Do nothing, it said.

The other German drained the last dregs from the wine bottle, drank it then belched loudly. For a moment or two he watched as his companion continued to fumble with Michelle's underclothes.

'For God's sake Jacob, if you're going to fuck her hurry up. We have to go.'

No, no. Not that. 'Ugh, urgh,' went Garnet. 'Ah, nn.'

'Sie ruhig, be quiet,' said Jacob. 'You want to know how is done? I show you.' And with that he jumped up and still holding Michelle, tripped her and threw her to the floor. She scratched and bit him only to have a fist punched into her head. Stunned and helpless she was forced to succumb while he broke the flimsy stuff of her pants and was at her.

Hands balled into fists Garnet roared. '*aaaaaaaah.*'

The pistol jammed into his throat was cold and hard. He closed his eyes. 'Open, open,' said Helmut. 'You watch and when he's done you watch me.'

Garnet froze. This was too much. Michelle had indicated that he was to do nothing, How could he do nothing when he was being made to watch what they were doing to her? But if he wanted them both to go on living he had to do as she said. So that he wouldn't cry out and tempt the man with the pistol to shoot them both he clamped his mouth shut, gritted his teeth, and turned his head away. Helmut's fist grabbed and held his chin and forced him to look at what Jacob was doing.

How long could this go on?

He would have to have revenge for this. Had to, had to strike back, had to inflict harm, any German soldier would do. He would demand the right to go with Laurent and the others on their night time forays. There had got to be something he could do, some way to seek revenge.

And then it was over. Taking the last of Michelle's wine and anything else they could lay their hands on, the two Germans went away laughing. Garnet pulled Michelle to her feet. Then he held her, held her close and tender. Tremors ran through her body, she buried her face in his chest and clung to him. His chin on the top of her head, he crooned softly to her while he rocked her gently back and forth as he would a baby, and there they stayed until she was ready to part from him. When she was she extricated herself from his arms very slowly. Keeping her head bent she turned away and would not look at him.

Her voice was cold and calculated when she said. 'They will pay. I will make them pay.' Then she went to wash and find clean clothes.

They did not talk again that day. Late into the night Garnet knew that Michelle had gone out. He could not sleep so waited for her to come home.

'The account has been settled,' she said when she did. 'There is nothing else to do. Go to bed, Pierre.'

Chapter 20

Garnet slept late. He thought Michelle must be sleeping too for he could hear no sounds of movement in her room. He moved quietly so as not to disturb her while he got his breakfast. When she was up he would try to help her put the traumatic events of yesterday behind her. He would treat her like a lady; show her that men were not all the same. Show her that she could trust him. He would do his best to repay her for being so kind. He would set the table for her. Maybe he could find a flower to put beside her plate. He looked into her china cupboard and found a small glass vase among the dishes. It was ideal, now he would see what flowers he could find. Snowdrops grew on the bank behind the apple tree, he had seen them yesterday. They were the ones he would pick. Pushing his feet into his outdoor shoes he opened the door and stepped out. Head bent as he walked he looked down at the grass that had been silvered by the slight frost that had come in the night. He looked up as he approached the apple tree.

'*Noooooooo,*' he screamed as he ran.

Michelle, head pushed sideways by the knot of the noose that encircled her neck, hung from the tree. The chair that she had used to reach the bough on which to tie the rope was lying on its side beneath her.

'*NO, NO, NO,*' shouted Garnet as he righted the chair and climbed up to cut Michelle down. Thank God he always carried a knife. She fell heavily against him. He lost his balance and they tumbled to the ground. She was limp and uncoordinated. But perhaps she'd done it wrong and there was still life in her body.

'I'm sorry, I'm sorry,' cried Garnet. He cradled her head and felt for a pulse. Nothing, tried again, still nothing. Gathering her lifeless body into his arms he held her tight, rocked back and forth and crooned to her amid a shower of tears.

'Why, Michelle, why did you do this? Why did you not talk to me? Oh God. What a waste.' Gradually the tears abated and he stopped rocking. 'We can't stay here. Let me get you indoors.'

He picked her up and carried her into her bedroom. He laid her down on fresh clean sheets; she had not lain in bed all night. Although he knew that it was too late he put his face close to hers hoping to feel a soft breath. There was none. And Michelle was cold. How long had she been hanging there? Why had she taken such a drastic step? Why had she not come to him for comfort? He would have cared for her as she had cared for him. Brushing her softly waving hair back from her face he smoothed the pillow beneath her head. He tidied her clothes to make it look as though she was lying there from choice. But there was nothing he could do about the angry marks around her neck. He kissed them, but they did not go away.

Garnet Plowman had never been one to pray, but he prayed now.

Dear God, please take this woman into your care and see that justice is done to those who caused her to take her own life. Amen.

He owed his life to Michelle. She had saved him from a slow death and now when she needed him most he had failed her. How was he ever going to put that right? While the sun continued on its daily course, while time swallowed the day, Garnet knelt beside her quiet body, but at last he raised himself up.

What was he to do? He was a stranger in a foreign land and there was no point in anything now that his guiding light had been extinguished. What he had done he had done for Michelle. She had not only saved his life but had given it meaning.

He went out of the house and into the garden and there before him was the apple tree, leafless now, but biding its time until the warm days of spring brought its buds into leaf. And there on the ground at its foot was the chair she had stood on, the chair she had kicked away . . .

He picked it up, swung it up over his head then with all the force he could muster smashed it again and again against the trunk of the tree. With every blow he cried. With every blow he swore in English and in French. With a splintering of wood the legs broke and fell. Again he bashed it against the tree and the seat, a circle of plywood, flew away. He swung once more. The rest of the flimsy wooden chair fell apart and he was left with only the back rest in his hands. He threw it away in disgust. With every blow he made he had mentally beaten the men who had abused the gentle woman who now lay lifeless on her bed.

'What are you doing, Pierre?'

Garnet swung around. Two men stood there. One was Laurent, the doctor who had treated him. He did not know the other. They had been watching him.

'Is something wrong?'

Oh no, nothing could be wrong. Only the most awful, dreadful thing that could happen has happened. The words came out of his mouth then in a bald statement. No flowery epithets. No sign of sympathy.

'Michelle is dead.'

'*Dead*!'

'Yes. The Germans came and drank her wine then they raped her and made me watch. They held a gun at my throat. I could do nothing and now she has hung herself.'

They followed him into the house and there beside Michelle's bed Garnet told them how it had happened, how he had been powerless to stop the soldiers. How he had been made to watch as in turn they used and abused her. Being unable to prevent it happening was something that was going to stay with him to the end of his days. 'God forgive me,' he said.

And then there had been the shock of finding her that morning when all he had been going to do was pick some snowdrops to put in a vase beside her plate at breakfast. He had wanted to cheer her up, wanted to be kind to her. And now he no longer could.

The doctor put his hand on Garnet's shoulder. 'You have nothing to blame yourself for. Michelle did what she did because she knew what might be in store for her later on. Not all are able to understand and forgive.'

'She went out somewhere that night. I couldn't sleep and was in the kitchen when she came home. She said that the account had been settled. And that I was not to ask. What did she mean?'

'All I can say is that she made them pay.'

'Thank you,' said Garnet. 'I want to avenge her death so I want to join you; in fact *I am* going to join you. I can operate and maintain field radios. If you won't have me I'll go by myself.'

'Ah no, do not do that. Your help would be most useful, but I could not make the decision on my own,' said Laurent. 'I will let you know. We will take care of our compatriot, it is our duty. You will have to live with one of us because you cannot stay here. We will put someone else in this house. Put any belongings you have in a bag then come with us.'

Belongings, what were they other than a spare shirt and underpants which Michelle had got for him? He dumped the bag that he put them in by his bedroom door, opened the door to Michelle's room and standing by her bed looked down at her. 'No more worries for you,' whispered Garnet. 'They cannot get you where you are now. God be with you.' He bent down to put a kiss on her forehead then abruptly turned away, picked up his bag and went into the garden to join the men.

Chapter 21

The fire sulked. It was raining. It was windy and the wind came from the quarter where it blew down the chimney and huffed smoke into the room. Luc was grizzly and irritable. He was sickening for something thought Dorrie. And Susan Jolliffe was right; at three years of age he was not content to be strapped in the pram while his mother worked. When he was out of it and on his feet he was into mischief. Maybe that was all right at home, but not when she was at the shop.

Dorrie sat at the table with a cup of tea in her hand. She stared at the window, at rain being thrown at it, at little rivers running down the glass. It had rained for several days and she had been unable to get out into the garden or do anything outside. Unable to settle she fretted at her confinement and paced the room. It wouldn't always be raining, but in a month or two it would be the start of winter with cold weather and perhaps snow. She still needed to gather enough kindling wood to last through the winter months. And what was she going to do about the bigger branches, the ones that had to be sawn into logs? She hadn't got enough of them yet. Last year the autumn had been fine and she'd managed, but things were different this year. But then, October might come in cold and crisp and dry and if she worked hard she would be able to gather together all the wood she would require, not only in October but maybe November too.

Perhaps she ought to think again about Lord Melchett's offer of going to live at Apsley Hall, if not for her then for Luc. She could cope with winter weather, but she was an adult, Luc was just a small child. Was she being selfish to insist on staying at the cottage? Life there was a continual battle to stay one step ahead, to provide food, to earn enough money to pay the bills and gather enough firewood to keep them warm.

She got up from the table and began to prepare some vegetables. With them and what was left of yesterday's rabbit stew there would be enough for their tea. If nothing else the rabbits that abounded on the common grazing, and the vegetables she grew, were plentiful so they would not go hungry.

She began to smile; it was not time to give in yet.

*

September rain had turned the ground into a sodden mess and just walking on it let alone pulling or carrying heavy pieces of wood was hard work. Gathering wood had to be put off until frost hardened the ground and made the going easier. So Dorrie took Luc by the hand and holding a small basket with his toy animals in went out to the barn. The wood she had already collected was stored there and this morning she planned to saw it into logs. She settled Luc in a safe place away from the saw bench, then placing a branch on the bench began to saw it up. Gradually as each log was cut and dropped to the ground a pile started to grow. Mid-morning Dorrie stopped. She was hot and thirsty.

'Come on, Luc,' she said. 'It's time for a drink and something to eat.'

Indoors she poured water from the pitcher. She cut a slice of cake for them both and when they had eaten and drank went back to her work. On the way she stopped to sit on Reuben's bench. She thought of Garnet. Was he ever going to come home? Had she made a rod for her own back by having a baby? She looked down at the child sitting by her side, put her arm round him hugged him and kissed the top of his head, his dark hair so like his father's and unlike hers. She was about to get up when she heard the sound of a car coming to a stop at the front of the house. Oh, please, not his lordship, she thought.

But it was.

Alasdair Carteret smiled to see her and put out his hand to ruffle Luc's hair. Luc brushed the hand away. 'He's wary of strangers,' explained Dorrie.

'I hope I won't always be that,' said Carteret. 'Now, have you decided when you are going to come and live with us?'

'Yes, and I'm not going to.'

There was a moment or two's silence before Carteret said, 'I would like to know your reasons, so can we go inside to discuss them?'

Reluctantly Dorrie led the way and when they were sitting either side of the table, Luc on Dorrie's knee, she said, 'There is no way I can come and live in your house. I wouldn't fit for a start. I mean, you only have to look at me to see that I don't belong. The servants would laugh at me.'

'My dear, your manner of dress has nothing to do with it. It is said that clothes make the man and I can provide you with whatever you require in that department.'

'It's not just the clothes. And in any case I don't have enough coupons for anything more than a coat.'

Carteret tut-tutted. 'In this life, Dorothea, anything and everything are available.'

'So would I be right in thinking that 'It's not what you know but who'?' said Dorrie. A shake of his lordship's head dismissed her remark. 'But even if you dressed me like a lady,' she went on, 'it wouldn't make any difference. I don't talk like you. I have a local accent. That would set me apart straight away and be an embarrassment both to me and to you.'

Alasdair Carteret gave a wry grin. 'Is there anything else you can think of to put in the way of my persuading you that I can offer you a better way of life?'

'I have to look after Leanacres. My mother and father worked hard to win a living from it and if I leave it, it will go to wrack and ruin.'

'I have to say I admire your determination.' Carteret leaned back in his chair. 'You get that from your mother. She left an easy life because she loved your father. I always thought that she would give up and come home, but as you know she never did. Was she happy with her choice?'

'I believe she was. She was lovely and I miss her *very* much.'

Carteret leaned forward and raised his voice to press his point. 'Then don't you think you owe it to her to take advantage of what I'm offering you? Wouldn't she want the best for you and your boy? I am trying to make amends for the wrong done to her. Can't you unbend a little and help me, if not for yourself then for your son?'

Of course Isobel would want the best for Luc, but not at the price his Lordship wanted her to pay. Hadn't she said in her letter that she wouldn't want Dorrie to try to find her family? There must be a reason.

'You seem to be hell bent on putting all the obstacles you can think of in the way,' went on Carteret. 'Come to us for the winter months. I don't like to think of you having to haul every drop of water you need and with only a wood fire to keep you warm. It's bad for your health.'

He isn't going to give up thought Dorrie, but she had grown up in this house, a house that was so cold in winter that ice made patterns on the inside of the windows, where she slept rolled up in blankets like a dormouse in its nest of leaves, till only the tip of her nose was showing. And she hadn't been ill.

'I'll think about it,' she said. 'But not until after I put the garden to bed.'

'Put the garden to bed, whatever do you mean?'

'I mean when all the vegetables that can be harvested have been and only cabbage and kale and a few leeks are left in the ground. Will that do?

'If you say so, Dorothea. Thank you, that will have to do.'

*

October obliged by sending the rain skittering away behind September, and when it had gone spread its own face wide in a sunny smile. It lit the dying leaves on the trees in the wood giving them a final few moments of glory. It coaxed the last of the roses on the climber beside Dorrie's door to lift up their heads and breathe out a sweet welcome when she came home from work.

'I suppose it won't be long before we have to start making plans for Christmas,' she said when a delivery of dried fruit arrived at the shop. 'Not that it makes a lot of work for me, but I don't like to see it pass by without something a bit special.'

'You'll come to us as usual, won't you?' said Susan.

'Wouldn't stay away for the world, you and your lot are my family now.'

'Good, that's how it should be. By the way, you've never said, but Bill Dewey's never bothered you again, has he?'

'I haven't seen hide nor hair of him. He's probably afraid to come into the shop since you threatened him with the broom.'

Susan laughed. 'He's a cheeky one. I don't suppose it bothered him. Maybe Farmer Mullins daughter's got him under control again. Let's hope so. Now then, here's another piece of news. We're getting evacuees. Apparently they're putting a woman and some kids in that cottage by the church. Wonder what they'll be like? Bet they don't stay long. I've heard they high tail back to the city because they can't stand the quiet of the country. Well, but it takes all sorts. Did you see where I put that receipt book?'

The day went on as most days did. Rosie came in.

'My golly, Dorrie, you started something when you got the WVS to organise knitting bee's didn't you?' she said.

'Why, what's happened?'

'Everybody's doing it. They meet up in one another's houses and have a high old time. My mum even tried to get me to have a go, but I couldn't be bothered with all them fiddly fingers on the gloves.'

'You could knit socks, couldn't you?'

'Well, yes, but then they've got heels.'

'You could bring your knitting up to my place and keep me company then I could turn the heel for you.'

'You're very persuasive, aren't you? All right then, I will. Mum can sit with the kids. When shall I come?'

The to and fro of customers still went on and kept Dorrie and Susan busy long after Rosie went home. Gossip was exchanged along with orders and receipts. News of who was ill, who had died, who had given birth and who had gone away was reported along with money or promises to pay at the end of the week.

'There's no need to buy the *Gazette* while you work in a shop, is there, Susan?' said Dorrie as she put her coat on ready to go home. 'All the local news comes through that door with the customers.'

'Very true,' said Susan Jolliffe. 'I'll see you tomorrow then.'

*

There was a slight chill in the evening air. Dorrie stepped out briskly. As she walked she talked to Luc and he chuckled and talked to her in his baby talk. At the common Moss was waiting. Dorrie opened the gate and pushed the pram through. She turned to close it and as she did a chill ran down her spine.

Bill Dewey was there on a bicycle. He stopped, got off, threw it against the bank then put his hand on the gate. He held it firmly and though Dorrie tried to close it against him she could not.

'Go away,' she said.

'Don't be like that darlin'. I told you I'd come to see you one day. This is it.'

'But I don't want to see you. Go away.'

Moss pressed close to Dorrie's side. The skin of her muzzle wrinkled and she exposed her teeth while a low growl rumbled in her throat.

'I don't know why you're being so stand offish,' said Bill. 'Are you like this with everybody? I only want to walk you home.'

'So you say, but I don't want you to. Can't you take no for an answer?'

He grinned. 'Aw, come on,' he said. 'I'm not going anywhere. If you don't let go of the gate I shall jump over it.'

She couldn't stop him. He came through the gateway and was beside her, much too close. Head and shoulders taller than she, he looked down at her and she felt intimidated.

'You're even prettier close up,' he said. 'Give us a kiss.'

'No, go away.'

But he caught hold of her, gripped her arms tight. 'I like a girl with a bit of fire in her, it makes things more interesting.' He pulled her towards him and bent his head to kiss her. Dorrie kicked, but his hold on her was strong, she was too close and there was no power in it, but all the same she still struggled.

'So you can kiss young Plowman, but not me, eh?'

Suddenly in one deft move Bill shifted his grip; slid one arm up her back, clamped his hand on her neck, held her head fast then fixed his mouth on hers. His lips were wet. Dorrie lifted her foot and raked the heel of her shoe down his shin.

'Aaagh,' yelled Bill as he let her go. She was almost free, but in that same moment his hand came out to deliver a stinging blow to her face. 'You're no angel just a bloody whore. Come here,' he grabbed for her again, and caught her. 'There's no point in you struggling. I'm going to share your bed tonight whether you like it or not.'

'No you aren't.'

'So would you rather lie in the open then? Watch the stars?'

The memory of her last night with Garnet flooded into Dorrie's mind. No way was she going to let Bill Dewey sully that so she attacked him. With feet and hands she kicked, punched and scratched. She shouted, she screamed and frightened by raised voices and aggression, Luc was reduced to tears. He bawled loudly and called for his mama.

'Shut up you little bastard,' yelled Bill.

'Don't you dare call him that,' shouted Dorrie.

'Aw, ha ha,' guffawed Bill. 'Sorry Darlin' but that's just what he is.'

Enraged Dorrie kicked, caught Bill on the shin, kicked and kicked again. Then there was a scuffle of feet a snarling dog and a yell from Bill as Moss bit him.

'Call him off, call him off,' shouted Bill as he lashed out at the dog.

'No, I'm not going to,' said Dorrie.

Moss hung on to Bill's trouser leg ready to strike again.

'You little bitch,' muttered Bill, 'if you're going to be like that Plowman's welcome to you. Now get that dog off me.'

'Leave Moss,' Dorrie said to the dog and to Bill Dewey, 'Go away; I don't ever want to see you again.'

'Nor me you.' Bill Dewey, his trouser leg flapping where Moss's teeth had ripped it, went through the gate, picked up his bike and road away.

Dorrie leaned over the pram, kissed her son and comforted him. 'It's all right, darling, it's all over,' she said.

Luc smiled at her through his tears and hiccupped as he sobbed.

Moss, tail switching madly, slipped her wet nose into the palm of Dorrie's hand. 'Well done,' said Dorrie as she patted her dog.

Chapter 22

'You've lost your shine, Dorrie, what's wrong?'

'Bill Dewey turned up when I was on my way home last night. I was really frightened. He said some awful things and he seized hold of me and said he wanted to sleep with me and I did what you said and kicked him. But then Moss bit him. Do you think he'll tell the police and will I be in trouble?'

'No, he got what he deserved. He won't say anything. PC Roberts knows all too well what he's like. But I've said it before and I'll say it again – you should *not* live up at Leanacres on your own.'

'But it's my home and I don't want to leave it.'

'That's as may be, but this is the second time you've been in danger, there was that German airman, remember? If you hadn't been out in the garden and saw him first goodness only knows what might have happened to you. And now you've been assaulted by Bill Dewey. Is there going to be a third time?'

'Whether there is or not, I don't want to leave Leanacres and that's another battle I have to fight. The village doesn't miss anything so I expect you know that *he* came to see me again.'

'You mean his Lordship. I did hear a rumour.'

Obviously agitated Dorrie twisted her hands together. 'He still wants me to go and live with them at Apsley. I told him that I hadn't any nice clothes and that I didn't talk like him and that I wouldn't fit in. But he said that didn't matter and then when I got home the other day a big box had been set down by my door. It was from him.' Dorrie paused. 'I ought to send it back.'

Susan Jolliffe was intrigued. Eagerly she asked, 'Why, what was in it?'

'Clothes,' said Dorrie. She hung her head. 'Beautiful clothes, but I haven't got enough coupons for them and you can't get clothes without coupons. So where did he buy them?'

'Huh, you shouldn't be surprised. It's well known that money will buy you anything and I don't suppose for a minute Lord Melchett is short of a few coppers. And it isn't only people like us that turn to crime, moneyed folk are no better. You've heard of the 'black market' haven't you?'

'Of course I have.'

'Well, there you are then, that's where he got them.' Susan went to the front of the shop where notices of forthcoming funerals, jumble sales and such were displayed in the window. 'Some of these will have to come down,' she said. She began to sort them out then stopped and said, 'Oh lor, here's Freda Plowman. Wonder what the dog's pinched now, and *don't* say she can have your cheese again my girl or she'll make a habit of it.'

The shop bell tinkled as Freda pushed open the door. 'Lovely weather,' she said. 'We can do with a bit of sunshine after all that rain.'

'And what can I get you today, Mrs Plowman?' asked Dorrie.

'Just a bit of flour, my love, I thought I might make some pancakes. And how's our boy?'

Freda tickled Luc under his chin and the little lad chuckled and reached up to her. She picked him up and held him. 'He's just like my Garnet was at that age. Wouldn't he be pleased to see him? What a day it will be when he comes home.'

'You haven't heard from him, have you?' said Susan.

'No. But France is full of Germans so he wouldn't be able to post a letter now would he. Could I take this little chap off your hands for an hour or two, Dorrie? I'd love to have him. Would you mind?'

'Not at all, I think that's a good idea. He can use the potty, but there's some clean stuff in the bottom of the pram just in case. Here's your flour.'

'So have you decided what you're going to do about going to Apsley?' asked Susan when Freda had gone and she and Dorrie went on with their work.

'I said I'd think about it and let him know when I'd put the garden to bed and couldn't work outside any longer, and then it was only a perhaps.' Dorrie was agitated and spoke sharply. 'I don't want to go, but on the other hand it seems silly not to. I just don't know what to do and I can't sleep at night for thinking about it.'

'Well I'd say that being set upon by Bill Dewey is a very good reason in favour of going, don't you? Or doesn't it bother you to think that he might try again?'

'I don't care if he does now that I know Moss will protect me. So don't go on at me Susan.'

Rosie opened the shop door, took one step inside, looked at Dorrie and Sue Jolliffe and said, 'Gosh, you two aren't having a row, are you? What's up?'

'Dorrie's got a problem,' said Susan. 'I don't know what she's dithering about. Perhaps you can help her sort it out 'cause I can't. It's time for our elevenses so you tell her, Dorrie, while I go and make a cup of tea.'

While Susan was busy in the kitchen Rosie sat on the chair by the counter. 'Now then,' she said, 'I'm all ears, what's it all about?'

'Well, the village knows that Lord Melchett has been to see me again so of course you do too. I hate to tell you, but it's turned out that he is a relative of mine. He's my uncle and he wants me to go and live with him and his family.'

Rosie's jaw dropped, then, open mouthed, she stared at Dorrie.

'My . . . God . . . Dorrie. I can't believe it . . . you . . .' for a moment words failed her then they came out in a rush. 'Why are you still here then? Why go on working in a shop? Why scrabble in the dirt like you do up at Leanacres? If I should be so lucky I'd be long gone. What's stopping you?'

'Leanacres is my home. You can take my place if you like because I'm quite happy where I am, thank you, and money can't buy happiness so I'd rather stay put.'

'Oh yes, and what about Luc? He's only little and you can manage on what you earn to keep you both just now, but as he gets bigger he's going to cost more and . . . well, we all know who his father is . . .but he isn't likely to come home, is he?'

Upset by Rosie's words Dorrie began to pace back and forth. 'We don't know that. Garnet's mum wasn't told that he was dead only that he was missing. And he might come home, you never know.'

'Come on, Dorrie. How long has he been gone, three years? Don't you think if he was still alive he would have been found by now? Or at least got a letter or something out to tell you he was all right?'

Tears filled Dorrie's eyes. 'France is full of Germans so how could anyone find him and what way do you think he could post a letter?'

Coming through from the back of the shop with mugs of tea Susan joined the conversation. 'Are you talking about Garnet? He could have been taken prisoner in which case he'd be in a concentration camp and if he was, Freda would know.'

'And like I said in that case he would have been able to get a letter to you,' said Rosie, 'but he hasn't. It doesn't look good, does it? I'm sorry if you think I'm being cruel but you have to face facts and life at Apsley Hall, even though you don't fancy it, has got to be better than where you are now.'

'I've been trying to tell her that,' said Susan. 'And there's another reason for her to leave. That Bill Dewey has been here a couple of times looking for her, and the other night he followed her home and really frightened her.'

'He didn't, did he?'

'He did. Moss bit him but I bet that won't put him off.'

'You're ganging up on me,' said Dorrie. 'I'm not going to go.'

Susan put her hands on Dorrie's shoulders and turned the girl to face her. 'Why don't you go there for a month or two and see how you like it. You said just now there wouldn't be much for you to do outside during the winter and you'd just as well be warm and snug in his house as your own. If you like being there you can stay, but if you don't you can come home and if you're lucky and Garnet does come back you can come home anyway.'

'I know that makes sense,' said Dorrie, 'but what am I going to do about Moss? I can't leave her at Leanacres on her own.'

Rosie laughed. 'Now she's worried about the dog. No problem, I'll have her.'

'I don't think she's got a leg to stand on now, do you Rosie?' said Susan. 'So you'll think about it then, Dorrie.' When Dorrie said she would she added, 'I suppose I shall have to advertise for another assistant soon. Would you like a job, Rosie?'

'I wouldn't say no.'

Chapter 23

It was a day of frost and a bitter wind when Dorrie finally locked the door of her house and allowed Lord Melchett's chauffeur to put the bags and boxes of things that she wanted to take with her into the boot of the car. She had not wanted to stop in the village to say goodbye to Susan so she had given her a spare key to Leanacres in case of emergency and had already taken leave of her. Moss was happily settled in with Rosie and her brood.

While Jenkins, the chauffeur, held the door open for her Dorrie lifted Luc into the back of the car then climbed in herself. She would not look back when they drove away. She had made her decision and right or wrong had to go with it.

The journey was uneventful. The soft seat and the motion of the vehicle soon had Luc curled up and asleep in the circle of his mother's arms. Dorrie gazed out of the window and remembered the other time she'd come that way. That day it had been a journey on a bus with Susan Jolliffe and it had been that day that led to this. That day they had entered the Hall through the back door. But it was not to be the back door this time and she gave a rueful smile when the car came to a stop at the front entrance. 'I will bring your luggage, Ma'am,' said Jenkins when Dorrie stood and gazed in awe at the impressive grandeur of the house.

The front door of Apsley, the biggest Dorrie had ever seen, was covered with black iron studs and door furniture. It opened and Lord Melchett stood there, a woman of perhaps forty years by his side. She was thin, her sandy hair looped up and tied with a ribbon. Dorrie stepped forward and the two came to meet her.

'You're here at last. Welcome to Apsley, my dear,' said Alasdair Carteret. This is your cousin, Georgina. Georgina this is Isobel's daughter, Dorothea.'

'Welcome to Apsley . . . Dorothea,' said Georgina. She smiled, if a sudden parting and spreading of the mouth and its sudden closure could be called a smile.

'Come along in and I'll get Lottie to show you to your room,' said Alasdair. 'Lunch is at one.'

Dorrie followed him into the house. The entrance hall was where the paintings were. She put Luc down then holding his hand stood and waited for the person called Lottie. Alasdair Carteret excused himself and went back to whatever he was doing in another room. Georgina looked Dorrie up and down then followed her father. As she slowly closed the door to the room they went into she peeped round it. What is the matter with the woman that she behaves so strangely thought Dorrie. The words in her mother's letter came to mind and her heart sank. They had brought her to this place, invited her in then abandoned her. That was not the way to behave.

The door to the servant's quarters and the door that Dorrie had come through by mistake, a mistake that had triggered this whole chain of events, opened and a woman in a white cap and apron came through. It was Lottie, the house maid, a plump middle aged woman. She smiled at Dorrie and said, 'I'm sorry to keep you waiting, ma'am. Has Jenkins carried up your bags?'

'I suppose he must have, I hadn't noticed.'

'If you would follow me then.'

Dorrie looked at the grand flight of stairs she was expected to climb. Luc would never manage it so she swept him up into her arms and followed the house maid.

'We put the little one's cot in your room,' said Lottie as she opened the door to Dorrie's bedroom. 'We thought that as everything would be strange to you both he would settle better if you were near.'

'That's very kind of you,' said Dorrie.

'The dinner gong will be rung ten minutes before lunch. It will give you time to get down to the dining room before it is served. His Lordship is very particular about family and guests being punctual at meal times. Is there anything else I can do for you?'

'I'm sure I'm going to get lost in this house so can you just tell me which was to go to the bathroom, please,' said Dorrie.

'Out of here, turn right and it's along at the end of the corridor. I'll leave you to settle in. Ring the bell if you need help with anything.'

When Lottie had gone Dorrie put Luc down on the floor and gave him one of his toys to play with while she took stock of her room. It was decorated in shades of green and white. Furniture in light grained wood was delicately fashioned, unlike the heavy durable furniture she had at home. She ran her fingers lightly over the top of her dressing table and loved the silky feel of its surface. She sat on the bed and bounced on it to test how firm it was. She lay on it, relaxed and because she had spent a sleepless night worrying whether she was doing the right thing, wished she could crawl under the covers and sleep there and then. But there was much to do, too many things to come to terms with to idle away time.

She stood up, walked to the window and looked out. An expanse of lawn that she judged to be as big as the two small paddocks at Leanacres put together sloped gently away from the house. Beyond it was a field and in it were cattle. She looked closer. Where was the fence that divided them from the lawn?

The sound of the dinner gong reverberated through the house. Dorrie scooped her son up from the floor, looked at him to make sure he was clean and dry then carried him back down the stairs and into the dining room. A high chair had been put next to the chair that she guessed was meant for her. She settled Luc then sat down. A sudden terror possessed her. On the table in front of her was a formidable array of cutlery. Who needed all these knives and forks and spoons? One knife, one fork and one spoon per person had been enough at home. How was she going to know which was the right one to use?

'I trust your room is to your liking,' said Alasdair Carteret as he took his place at the head of the table.

'It's lovely,' said Dorrie.

Georgina had obviously thought that a change of clothes was demanded and, clad in a chiffon dress, she floated into the room and took her place opposite Dorrie. Luc sat quietly by her side and Dorrie thought of Susan who said she was lucky to have such an amenable child.

Lunch arrived. It was soup. A parlour maid, also in a white cap and apron, but this time a lacy affair, served Lord Melchett first, then Georgina, then her and a small dish for Luc. Dorrie stared at the thick brown liquid. It was not like the soup she made at home where small pieces of vegetable floated and were recognisable. And which spoon should she use? She looked up and across the table at Georgina who smiled and held up the spoon she was using, gave it a little wiggle then went back to her soup. Dorrie gave a sigh of relief. That was the first hurdle cleared. When she and Luc were finished she put down her spoon, wiped her mouth with the napkin by her plate, folded it and put it down then started to get up.

'I think we have cold meat and salad today,' said Georgina. 'Do you like salad?'

'Yes, oh yes, I do,' said Dorrie.

Hoping that Lord Melchett had not noticed her wrong move Dorrie sat down again. They waited then for their plates to be cleared, waited again for clean plates to arrive and again for the salad. What a long time this meal is taking thought Dorrie. When it was finally done she excused herself on the pretext that Luc needed to take a nap. It wasn't really an excuse because when she laid him in the cot it was only a few seconds before he was asleep.

She unpacked the things she had brought with her and put them away and now there was nothing to do. She had forgotten her knitting and her hands, once so busy, were idle. I haven't been here five minutes, I don't know what to do with myself and I'm bored. If this is supposed to be a better life then I don't think I like it. I hope it's going to improve.

It did not. Dorrie stayed in her room. When Lottie knocked on her door and told her that tea and sandwiches were being served in the morning room, she thanked her and refused them. When it was time for dinner she left Luc, who she had fed earlier and who was asleep, in his cot while she went down. Dinner, like lunch, was a lengthy affair. Afterwards she pleaded a headache and escaped again to her room. She slept fitfully and in the morning thought that at some time during the night she had heard music and someone singing, but dismissed it and thought she must have been dreaming.

Chapter 24

The December morning was cold and crisp. Dorrie woke rested and refreshed. What new experience was this day going to bring? Washed and dressed she got Lucas ready and went down to breakfast. When she walked into the dining room a strange man stood by the sideboard. He was helping himself to food. Her eyes opened wide when she saw that the plate in his hand was piled high with bacon, eggs and sausages.

He turned and saw her. 'Hello,' he said. 'You must be my cousin Dorothea. I've heard about you. I'm Jocelin, but you can call me Joss. And who is this?' He smiled at Luc.

'This is Lucas,' said Dorrie. She took the hand that Jocelin Carteret held out to her and when it was taken found hers held in a firm grip. Jocelin, considerably taller than Dorrie, smiled down at her.

'You have to help yourself to breakfast,' he said. 'There's plenty there, have as much as you like.'

Dorrie put Lucas in his chair and gave him a rusk to chew on while she got breakfast for them both. She picked up a plate then looked into the dishes that held the food. There was enough there for a dozen people she thought. She chose bacon and egg for herself and porridge for Luc. "There's plenty there, have as much as you like." Joss had said. But where did it all come from? Rations for four people were not enough to provide a spread like that.

Georgina, dressed in riding clothes, strode into the room.

'Ha, little brother,' she boomed, 'when did you get back?' She threw an arm round Jocelin and gave him a kiss. 'It's a grand morning for a ride. Are you going to come with me? The mare needs exercising. '

'I don't think so,' said Joss.

'What about you, Dorrie? Do you ride?'

'No, I don't.'

'Have to teach you then. I'm sure we can find an old nag that would suit you.'

Not if I can help it thought Dorrie.

It seemed that breakfast was a casual affair. Though food was kept warm in heated dishes on the sideboard, but late comers would have to be content with food that was not as hot as they would like. Lord Melchett was last to arrive.

'Good morning, good morning,' he said. 'I trust you slept well, Dorothea. Have you any plans for today?'

'Not really,' said Dorrie. 'I did think that I might have a look at your vegetable plot though.'

Jocelin laughed. 'Plot! I think you'll find it's rather more than that. But old Burt Maidment will be only too happy to show you round.'

Breakfast over Dorrie took Luc to see the portraits in the hall.

'Look at this one,' she said. 'It's a picture of your grandmother.'

Luc held a hand out towards it, 'Mama,' he said. Then he looked at his mother and, with puzzlement in his voice he repeated, 'Mama.'

'No darling,' said Dorrie. 'It's my mama, your grandmamma.'

Jocelin came up behind her. 'You can't blame him,' he said. 'You are exactly like her.'

Maybe,' said Dorrie. 'Who are all the others?'

'They're mostly family, that's Aunt Persephone and there's Uncle Bradshaw, he was nice. That's Great Aunt Lilith and this one is our Grandmother, Lady Davinia Carteret. She looks quite fierce, don't you think?'

That was putting it mildly thought Dorrie as she gazed at a face in which steel grey eyes seemed to bore deep into her very soul. She shuddered. The nose was thin and the chin pointed. It was the face of a wasp. Unlike bees that could sting only once a wasp could sting and sting again. And Dorrie knew that that was what this woman had been capable of.

'I don't like her,' she said.

'Not many people did,' said Jocelin. He moved on to the next portrait. 'And this is Henry George Carteret, grandfather.'

In contrast to his waspish wife, Henry George looked down his aquiline nose in a very condescending manner. If he was still here I wouldn't be thought Dorrie. I can see that he'd treat me as nothing more than the muck on his shoes. 'I don't think I want to look at any more,' she said.

'Nor me,' said Jocelin. 'Do you want to go and look at the vegetable plot now?' He laughed.

'Why not, it's a nice morning.'

'Come with me then. I'll show you the way. You can have a look at the front garden while you're at it.'

Dorrie followed him through the hall to the drawing room. He opened glass doors that led out on to a paved area. Garden chairs and tables suggested that it was the ideal place for after dinner drinks. A wide gravelled walk lay between it and a wide expanse of lawn and flower beds.

'My bedroom must be on this side,' said Dorrie. 'I looked out of the window and

this is what I could see. But there are cattle in the fields down there.' She pointed to where the fields seemed to be a continuation of the lawn. 'I can't see any fence so how do you keep them out of the garden?'

'Easy. The ha-ha does that.'

'The ha-ha, what's that? Or are you making fun?'

'It's a wide ditch with a fence at the bottom of it. It's called a ha-ha because, ha-ha,' Jocelin laughed, 'you can't see it.'

The scrunch of a horse's hoofs made Jocelin and Dorrie turn to see what was coming, and there was Georgina on a horse that was big and black trotting along the gravel path towards them.

'Why the stallion, Georgy?' said Jocelin.

'You've only got to look to see why. He's dying for a gallop.'

That would be right thought Dorrie for the horse, its coat gleaming like silk, was restless. Never still, all four of its feet were constantly in action, it danced while its eyes rolled and showed the whites. It snorted and blew froth from its nose.

'Be quick, saddle up and come with me, Joss. I'll race you.'

'No, Georgy. Not today,' said Jocelin.

'Aw come on do.' Jocelin shook his head. 'Oh well, can't waste time and if you're not coming I'll be off.' Georgina pulled the horse's head round, spurred him and sent him galloping off across the lawn, leaping flower beds and sending up divots of earth as he went.

Dorie gasped. 'What's she doing? She's ruining the garden. Oh my God, she'll be killed. That horse is dangerous. Oh, I don't want to look.'

'Never fret, little cos,' laughed Joss. 'She'll jump the ha-ha, she's done it before. Just watch.'

'But, but . . .'

Georgina, at one with the stallion, rode like a devil. Tail up and streaming like a pennant, the horse sped towards the hidden fence, the wide ditch. Dorrie put her hands over her face, fingers spread to peep through. She held her breath as the pair reached the fence and took off. They flew. The stallion, front legs stretched forward to anticipate contact with the ground on the opposite side of the ditch, back legs drawn up ready to connect and push off, sailed through the air. And then they were down and galloping on. Dorrie gave a sigh of relief.

'Told you, didn't I,' said Jocelin. 'She's mad, you know, quite mad, but harmless as long as she doesn't forget to take the pills.' Mad? Surely he was joking. 'Dad's not going to be pleased. She's made a mess of the lawn and Maidment will threaten to resign . . . again.' Joss dissolved into laughter. 'What a life. Are you sure you did the right thing by coming to live with us?'

'I'm beginning to wonder,' said Dorrie.

'Get your coats and I'll show you the way to the garden,' said Jocelin.

The kitchen garden at Apsley Hall was enormous. Access to it was by way of a vast arched entrance in the ten foot high wall that surrounded it. Paths wide enough for a horse drawn cart dissected individual plots. Dorrie's eyes grew round as she gazed in awe at the immaculate ranks of vegetables. There were also plots that contained nothing but fruit bushes.

'Have you lost your tongue, Dorothea?' said Jocelin.

'Who wouldn't when faced with this? It's enormous. No wonder you laughed when I said I wanted to see your vegetable plot. Why is it so big?'

'This is a typical garden for a country house. Normally there would be a lot of people to cater for. The house once used to be full of them. There were house parties and dinner parties. A lot of famous people sat at our table. But the war stopped all that when rationing was introduced.'

But rationing hasn't made much of a dent in your larder thought Dorrie. She carried Luc astride her hip. He was getting too heavy to be carried any other way. She put him down to walk.

'We'd better find Maidment,' said Jocelin. 'You'll get lost and never find your way out otherwise. Lunch is always at one o'clock. Do you have a watch?'

'No.'

'Then I'll get you one, but Maidment will know the time so don't be late. Here he is now.'

A man wearing dark clothes and a broad brimmed hat touched his forelock when he saw Jocelin Carteret. 'Morning, sir,' he said.

'I've brought you a visitor, Maidment,' Jocelin said to the gardener. 'She wants to look at your 'vegetable plot'. I'll leave you now, Dorothea. Enjoy yourself.'

'So are you interested in gardening ma'am?' asked Maidment.

'Yes, I am,' said Dorrie.

'Follow me then, and I'll show you what we do here.'

With Luc toddling by her side Dorrie walked behind the head gardener. She listened when he told her the names of plants, which varieties he liked best, which ones he did not. They wandered among beds of winter cabbage, Musselburgh leeks and Brussel sprouts. On to strawberries beds, lines of raspberry canes, and then to apple trees and pear trees trained along the garden wall. Finally they came to the hothouses where he showed her grape vines, a fan trained apricot, and a small tree that they expected would bear oranges.

At the end of the tour Dorrie said, 'It's such a big garden for so few people. You must grow much more than is needed so what happens to the surplus?'

'It's sold to traders in the town. They come out and collect it. I don't know the financial arrangements, but the money for it must go some way to paying for heating the greenhouses and for new seed and stuff. Not that we need much seed, we do save our own.'

'As I do,' said Dorrie. 'Thank you for showing me your garden, Mr Maidment, I've found your talk very interesting.'

'It's been a pleasure, ma'am.'

Chapter 25

During the night snow had fallen and next morning Dorrie looked out of her bedroom window on a land that had been transformed. The lawns and the fields beyond were carpeted in white. Any remaining flowers had, along with shrubs and bushes, been converted into weird shapes. There would be no long walks with Luc in his pushchair around the estate today; it would be an indoor day, a day to curl up with a book. She would see what was available in the room where the walls were lined with them. When she had settled her son in his cot for his morning nap she went downstairs. Every day she noted things that were so very different from those at home. Floors there were of flag stones or bare wood. Other than the rag rug in her bedroom there were no carpets and thus no way was it possible to tread silently. Here floors were covered with carpets and rugs and footfalls made no sound.

When she drew near the library Dorrie could hear the murmur of voices and recognised those of Jocelin and Georgina. At first what was being said was indistinct but as she got closer the words became clear.

'What's she doing here, Joss? Why did father have to pick her up? It would have been better for her and for us if he'd left her where she was.'

'Be fair, Georgy. She didn't ask to come and she's not asking for anything so you've nothing to complain about.'

'It's not just that,' said Georgina. 'She doesn't know anything. She can't ride, doesn't play bridge, I doubt if she's ever had a proper education and she doesn't even know which knife and fork to use. She doesn't belong here.'

The door to the library was partly open. Dorrie forbore to push it wider. They were talking about her. What else was Georgina going to say?

'And I couldn't very well introduce her to my friends could I?' her cousin went on. 'She talks like one of the servants; in fact she's no better than them. And have you seen her hands? She's got the hands of a peasant. The kitchen and the servants' hall is where she belongs, not here with us.'

'Come on, Georgina, you're being much too harsh. She's only been here five minutes. She needs time to adjust.'

At least Jocelin was defending her.

'Well, she might be an imposter,' said Georgina. 'Had you thought of that?'

'You have only got to look at her mother's portrait to know that's not true. Dorothea could be the one who sat for the painting. And I'm sure father had his solicitor confirm that she was who she said she was. He would never have brought her here otherwise. So you'll just have to accept it. You don't have to become bosom friends but you could be nice to her couldn't you? It'll cost you nothing.'

'No, I can't, she makes me feel uncomfortable.'

'And uncharitable too, for goodness sake you could at least try. Now get lost. I want to use the phone.'

Dorrie moved quickly and slid quietly into the drawing room. It was never or very rarely used in the morning so there would not be anybody there. With the door slightly ajar she waited and listened until there were no voices, and hoping that Georgina had gone she opened the door and peeped out. There was no one in the hall or on the staircase. All was clear. She stepped out and pulled the door shut behind her. She was just about to walk away when she heard Jocelin's voice. He was speaking in a very conspiratorial way, up to no good she thought, and hesitated.

'I can't get you a whole carcase, half will have to do . . . no, you can't come here to collect it. I'll phone you and give you a time and place to meet up.'

I don't want to hear any more and books will have to wait thought Dorrie. Something's going on that I don't want to know about.

Luc was sleeping soundly when she crept back into her bedroom. So as not to wake him she sat on the bed and twiddled her thumbs. No book to read, no knitting to do, and even the weather had turned against her. Somehow she had to get out of the house and if nothing else buy some knitting wool and needles. Why hadn't she thought to put some in her bag to bring with her?

There was a light tap on the door, the handle creaked and the door opened. Dorrie turned to see who was coming. Lottie's face peeped round it.

'I'm so sorry Ma'am,' she said when she saw Dorric. 'I was just looking to see if I could clean and I didn't want to wake the baby if he was asleep.'

'Please come in,' said Dorrie. 'I wonder if you can help me. Is there a shop within walking distance? There are things I want, wool and knitting needles in particular, and unless someone takes me to the town I don't know where to get them.'

'There's a general store in the village. It's got wool and a bit of everything else and it's the Post Office as well. Too far to walk but if you can ride a bike you could borrow mine.'

'Oh, could I really? Ah, but what would I do with Luc?'

'I'd look after him. We have a couple of hours off in the afternoon and I'm quite used to little children. I have enough nephews and nieces. It would be a pleasure.'

It would also be my pleasure thought Dorrie. The chance to ride a bicycle again and be free and unfettered and away from the constraints of Apsley Hall would be bliss.

'I would love to borrow your bike,' said Dorrie.

*

When most of the snow had melted and roads were clear, Dorrie accepted the loan of Lottie's bike and set off for the village and the shop. The lanes were narrow but petrol rationing kept many cars off the road so Dorrie pedalled happily along. She was delighted when the road went down a hill. She laughed as with gathering speed the wind plucked at her coat tails, lifted them and flapped them like the wings of a bird, ran its fingers through her hair and tingled colour into her cheeks. She stuck her legs out above the racing pedals and rejoiced in the freedom Lottie's bike had given her. But she was coming to the village. She pulled on the brakes, searched for and found purchase on the pedals and brought the bicycle to a stop by the village shop. She got off, leaned the bicycle against a wall, then walked up a couple of steps and into the shop.

'Afternoon,' said the woman behind a counter. 'What can I get you?'

'I'd like some writing paper, envelopes and stamps and do you have any knitting wool?' asked Dorrie.

All o' those is over there,' said the woman. She pointed to the back of the shop. 'There's needles and patterns too. Pick what you want while I get your stamps.'

Dorrie selected wool for a scarf and for a jumper for Luc. She also chose a pattern and two pairs of needles. She then chose a writing pad and some matching envelopes, bundled it all together and took it to the shop counter.

'I'll need some clothing coupons for this,' said the woman indicating the wool. 'Have you got your book?'

Dorrie had and the woman clipped the appropriate coupon from it and asked if that was all Dorrie wanted. It was. The cost totted up, Dorrie paid and with her purchases in a bag thanked the woman and left the shop. A basket was clipped to the handlebars of the bicycle. Dorrie put the bag with the things she'd bought into it, got on the bike and rode away.

At Apsley Hall she let herself in and following the sound of Luc's laughter found him in the servant's hall with Lottie and the parlour maid.

'Mama,' he cried when he saw her. He held out his arms. Dorrie put her bag of purchases on the table and picked him up.

'I hope he's been good,' she said. 'Thank you for looking after him and for the loan of the bike.'

'He's a darling and we've loved having him,' said Lottie. 'I hope you'll let me look after him again.'

'I'd be only too pleased if you would.'

'You're in time for afternoon tea,' said the parlour maid. 'I've just taken it into the morning room.'

Afternoon tea was a pernickety tit-bit thought Dorrie. It annoyed her. In fact the whole routine of life at the Hall annoyed her. It all seemed so pointless and she longed to be able to do something useful.

'Have you had a nice day, Dorothea?' asked Georgina as she reached for a paste sandwich.

'Yes, thank you,' said Dorrie.

'That wasn't you I saw on a bicycle, was it?'

'I daresay it was.'

'Heavens, what on earth made you want to ride a bicycle? Where did you get it?'

'I borrowed the one that belongs to Lottie. I had nothing to do and I was bored. I'd forgotten to bring my knitting so I asked her where I could get wool and needles. She told me where I could and offered to lend me the bike.'

'I will take you anywhere you want to go,' said Alasdair Carteret. 'You do not need to hob-nob with the servants. Why did you not ask me?'

'I thought that you wouldn't want to use your petrol ration just to take me to the shop. I know it limits you as to how far you can go and there was no need to use the car when the bike was free.'

Knuckles rattled on the door, it opened and Lottie stepped in. 'I do beg your pardon M'Lord, but Mrs Carter has had an accident.'

'An accident, what has she done?' Lord Melchett put down his cup of tea. 'Blast,' he said as he got up. 'I'd better come and see I suppose'.

In the kitchen Mabel Carter sat and cradled her arm.

'Now Mrs Carter, what have you been up to? Been at the cooking sherry and had a tumble eh?' It was Alasdair Carteret's attempt to bring a smile to the woman's face. It nearly succeeded. 'What have you done?'

'I think I've broken my wrist.'

'Then we'd better get you to the hospital. Jenkins will take you.'

'Someone must go with her,' said Dorrie.

'I will,' said Lottie.

'Very well,' said Carteret. 'I'll ring for Jenkins.' He strode away.

'Someone will have to take your place, Mrs Carter,' said Dorrie. 'And I think it's going to be me. What you had planned for dinner?'

'There's a casserole in the oven, but potatoes and veg need to be got ready. There's a fruit pie in the larder. You need to make some custard to go with it. But *you* shouldn't be doing that.'

'Well, who else is going to?' said Dorrie. 'Lottie's coming with you and Miss Scammel has to see to the table and serve.'

'Now, now, Mrs Carter, what have you been up to?' said Jenkins as he bustled into the kitchen. 'Are you ready? Shall we go?'

'No,' said Dorrie. 'Her arm needs a support. Someone find me a towel or a cloth or something.'

'I've got a scarf,' said Lottie. She ran to fetch it then handed it to Dorrie.

'That'll do.' Dorrie arranged the scarf to support Mabel's arm. 'You'll have to help hold it up with your other arm too,' she said. 'Now you'd better go and get sorted out. See you soon. And don't worry, you'll be all right and we'll manage.'

We'll manage. Hm. Mabel Carter was going to be out of action for several weeks. In a few day's it would be Christmas. There wasn't much sign of it in Apsley Hall. No one had put up decorations and no Christmas tree had appeared. Was it taboo in this house? Surely they would have a traditional Christmas dinner, but if one was planned who was going to cook it? A bad feeling settled on Dorrie. Was that job going to be hers as well?

Chapter 26

Mabel Carter did not return to Apsley Hall to supervise the preparation of dinner so Dorrie had no option but to see to it. Leaving the pie and a jug of custard for the parlour maid to deal with she joined the rest of the family in the dining room.

'This really is a delicious casserole, Dorothea,' said Alasdair Carteret.

'Praise for it should go to Mrs Carter, not me,' said Dorrie.

'Ah, but for you it would never have got to the table,' said Georgina. 'You have found your place in this house, Dorothea. The kitchen certainly seems to be where you belong, It suits you very well.'

'I will not have you talk to your cousin like that, Georgina. Dorothea belongs here with us and you are being unkind,' said her father. 'We should be very grateful to Dorothea for stepping in and filling a gap that no one else could.'

'But of course,' simpered Georgina. 'And I am grateful, but I must say that you are an excellent cook, Dorothea. Perhaps we should employ her, father.'

'Georgina this is not the time or place to talk to Dorothea in that way. I did not ask your cousin to come and live with us to treat her as a servant. She deserves better and you should do your best to make her welcome.'

'Yes, papa,' said Georgina.

But while her father concentrated on his food Georgina, head bent, a sardonic look on her face, gave a sideways glance at Dorrie.

"Harmless as long as she keeps taking the pills." That was what Jocelin had said. So perhaps, thought Dorrie, he was right in implying that Georgina was mad. And perhaps it was the possibility of madness being inherent in her family that had made Isobel write that letter and in it indicate that she did not want her daughter to try to find them. And now, all because of that accidental meeting, she was here in their midst.

'Have any plans been made for Christmas Day?' asked Dorrie.

'We do not make much of the festival,' said Alasdair Carteret. 'There are not enough of us to mark the celebration any more. I'm afraid the Carteret line is dying out and my offspring are not helping in the matter.'

So I'll take that as a no thought Dorrie.

When dinner was over, when the dishes had been cleared away and washed up and when Mabel Carter, her broken wrist in plaster, had been welcomed back, fussed over and put to bed, Dorrie went to her own room. She was tired and was looking forward to a good night's sleep. She had promised to make breakfast and would have to get up early to light the coal fired kitchen range. But before she got into bed she must write a letter to Susan. She pulled a chair up to her dressing table and began.

Dear Susan,

Luke and I are well. The living here is very different to what I have been used to. I am finding it difficult to fit in. There are such a lot of things I don't know. Oh, I must tell you ,your sister has broken her wrist. Some hot fat got spilled on the kitchen floor; she slipped on it and fell. I have had to take over some of the cooking though I think they are going to get a temporary help. Christmas is likely to be a very sober affair and I wish very much that I could be at home with you.

I hope you and your husband are well. Give my regards to Garnet's mum when you see her.

Love,

Dorrie. X x

The letter folded and put into an envelope, she addressed it and stuck on a stamp. She would put it on the tray on the hall table for the postman to collect or for someone to post if they were going out.

When that was done, Dorrie had a bath to wash away the dust of the day, put on her nightdress, slid between crisp cotton sheets, and with a soft pillow under her head sank under the comfort of warm blankets and eiderdown. She closed her eyes and relaxed, drifted into the never land of slumber, smiled to hear the tinkling music of the fairies, the sweet songs that they were singing. But then the singing got louder, the music too, and a voice telling someone not to be so silly.

Not to be silly? Dorrie sat up and threw back the bedclothes. The music was still playing. It was coming from the garden. She went to the window and looked out. Cavorting on the lawn was Georgina. Leaving nothing to the imagination she wore a diaphanous gown and not much else. It was Georgina who was singing. There were no fairies and however much she tried Georgina was never going to look like one. She was tall, leggy and uncoordinated, a colt not long born trying out its legs.

A figure stepped out from the shadow of the house – Jocelin, the man who was master of disappearing and reappearing. When did he come home? The music was still playing, but where was it coming from? Dorrie opened the window and leaned out. On one of the patio tables there was a record player. Jocelin went to it, switched it off and closed the lid. When the music stopped Georgina came to an abrupt halt. Balling her hands into fists she shook them at Jocelin. 'You beast,' she cried.

'I am, aren't I?' said Jocelin. 'Come and tell me what's been happening while I've been away.'

A wide smile spread across Georgina's face.

'You're a naughty boy to go away and leave me on my own.' To join him she hopped across the gravel path grabbed his arm and began to talk rapidly, but she had lowered her voice and Dorrie could hear nothing but a murmur. They were moving back into the house.

What on earth possessed Georgina to go out on a winter night so scantily dressed? She was asking for pneumonia. The more Dorrie saw of her cousin the more she thought that if not actually mad Georgina was at least mentally unstable. Was this why the Carteret family were dying out? The same could not be said of Jocelin, for he appeared to be very fit. He was also very clever in his handling of the oddity that was his sister. Dorrie closed the window and went back to bed.

She was in the kitchen clearing up after breakfast next morning when Jocelin popped his head round the door. 'Can you come and give me a hand, Dorothea?' How she wished they wouldn't keep calling her that. It was her name but she much preferred to be called Dorrie.

'Yes, all right, but you'll have to wait a minute or two.'

She found him in the drawing room surrounded by boxes. A small fir tree lay on the floor. 'My goodness, what's this?' she said.

'It's a Christmas tree. I got it for Luc. I want you to help me put it up, but you will have to decorate it.'

'And what's your father going to say? It seems he has no time for Christmas.'

Jocelin smiled. 'There won't be much he can say when it's up and trimmed eh?'

There was nothing for it but to do as he asked. Maybe Christmas wasn't going to be so bad after all. Dorrie had not been looking forward to it and had been wishing that she could be back in the village with the Jolliffes, sitting at their table and sharing their Christmas dinner. There wouldn't be a lot of room round the table for Susan's daughter in law and children would be there. But it would be warm and welcoming and there would be a glass of wine and lots of laughter, unlike the chill correctness of Apsley Hall.

When the tree had been put up, when the box of decorations had been opened and used to dress it and when Jocelin had put holly and ivy around the fireplace and pictures he said, 'There's just one more thing, presents to go under the tree.'

'Presents? But I haven't got any. I thought about it but . . .'

'You didn't know what to give to father. Never mind, I have some for you.'

'Why are you being so kind to me, Jocelin?'

'Because I get the feeling you are not happy here. Am I right?'

'I'd rather not talk about it. I must go and check on Luc and then get lunch.'

Dorrie ran up the stairs and along to her room. She knew Lucas was awake. She could hear him crying and that was strange because he was usually happy when he woke. Thinking that she had left him too long she burst into the room. Crouched by the side of the cot was Georgina. She was growling and screwing up her face. When Luc wailed she laughed and twisted her face again.

'What on earth do you think you are doing?' cried Dorrie. 'Are you mad?'

She ran to Luc, picked him up and soothed him. Luc clung to her and sobbed.

'Don't be silly. He loved it and I was having fun.'

'You may have been, but you were frightening him. Couldn't you see that he was terrified? Leave him alone. Go away.'

'Rubbish. Treat 'em rough and make 'em strong. You don't want a milk sop of a child do you?'

'No more than I want a child cowed into submission,' said Dorrie.

'He'll never be a leader if you don't teach him how to take the knocks and come up smiling.'

'He doesn't have to be a leader. I hope that he'll find his own station in life. But it won't be by being bullied into doing something he doesn't want to.'

Georgina shrugged and pulled a face. 'All right,' she said. 'I think you're wrong but have it your own way, I'm going.' Georgina made a face at Luc and slammed the door as she went out.

*

'You're a very bad patient, Mrs Carter,' said Dorrie when, with Luc settled in a play pen in a corner of the kitchen, she began to prepare lunch. Though handicapped by the plaster on her arm it was impossible to stop Mabel from fetching and carrying.

'You are a guest,' she said to Dorrie, 'you shouldn't have to work.'

'But it's Christmas, where are you going to find temporary help? I'm here and I can do it. Tell me this, where does all this food come from? I've totted up ration books and you don't have enough for what I see you putting on the table.'

'Ah, best you don't ask.'

'Stop stalling. I'm not blind you know.'

Mabel Carter put the dish she was carrying on the table, stared at it for a moment or two then looked directly at Dorrie. 'It's Master Jocelin,' she said. 'I don't ask him where or how he gets it. But he can get anything you want and no questions asked.'

So that's where all my new clothes came from. He's a crook. I ought to report him. But wouldn't that be biting the hand that feeds me?

Dorrie looked at Mabel Carter, at the worried frown on her face.

'Cheer up,' she said. 'I'm not going to say anything. Now, what do you want me to do next?'

Lunch was ready on time but Georgina was not. Just as the parlour maid was serving soup the sound of a horse's hooves on the gravel path and the excited whinny of a horse could be heard. Georgina was doing her own thing . . . as usual.

Alasdair Carteret stood up, roared and shouted, 'God help us. Go and tell that woman to put that blasted horse away, Jocelin.'

'Waste of time father. As soon as she sees me she'll be gone.'

'I've had enough of her stupid childish pranks. I'll have the beastly animal shot. Perhaps that'll teach her a lesson.'

Jocelin went on taking his soup. Quite calmly he said, 'No father, you won't. Surely you know how much that animal is worth. It's too valuable to shoot, but you could put it up for sale.'

Dorrie looked from father to son. It was not just Georgina who was mad she thought. The whole family seemed to have been tarred with the same brush. So why had Isobel not been the same? Was it because different blood flowed in her mother's veins? Was it because her mother had been of different stock? And was this odd behaviour in Alasdair Carteret's family the reason why Isobel said she didn't want her daughter to look for or find her relatives?

Chapter 27

'We really don't need this,' said Georgina as she tossed a dismissive gesture in the direction of the Christmas tree. 'Christmas is for babies and with the exception of the brat here, we are all adult.'

'That remark was uncalled for, Georgina, and I am losing patience with you,' said her father. 'Dorothea and her child are members of our family and deserve to be treated with respect. Jocelin has organised a celebration for the little one. You should follow his example. If you can't do that and be sociable you had better leave us and go to your room.'

'No father, I am not going to do that. I am not the intruder.' Georgina pointed a finger at Dorrie. 'She is.'

'She is not an intruder, she is your cousin,' snapped Alasdair Carteret. 'She is my guest and you will treat her in the same manner you would any other.'

'I'm sorry father, but neither you nor I hob-nob with the servants, which is what Dorothea has been doing. She didn't like it when I tried to amuse the child yet she happily leaves it in the servant's hall for them to look after. Why does she do that? I will tell you. It is because that is the class to which she belongs. Why did you have to bring her here? You should have left her where she was.'

The spirit of Christmas is definitely not alive in this house, thought Dorrie. She glanced at Jocelin. As he listened to the conversation between his father and Georgina his gaze swivelled from one to the other.

'Calm down, Georgie,' he said. 'Christmas is for children and lasts only a day. Surely you can unbend enough to let the child have a little happiness?'

But Georgina was not to be stopped. 'Well, if you want people to be happy perhaps I should go and collect the cook, the housemaid and parlour maid, and ask them to join us. You could pass round the wine and mince pies, Joss. What about the gardener too and . . . aaah,' Georgina, a demonic grin on her face leaned towards Dorrie, 'I'm forgetting the stable boy. Oh yes, of course. The stable boy, that's it, isn't it. Our little cousin here is his spawn.'

'*Enough*,' shouted Carteret as he sprang from his chair. 'I will *not* tolerate your behaviour. It is not becoming to you. Leave us . . . *now*.'

'No.' Georgina leaned back in her chair and crossed one leg over the other. The grin on her face had changed to a smile of satisfaction.

Luc, who was upset by Georgina's aggressive voice, clung to his mother's skirt and whimpered. Dorrie picked him up. He wrapped his arms tightly round her and buried his face in her neck.

'I am so sorry, Dorothea,' said Carteret.

'Don't be,' said Dorrie. 'My mother taught me that it was possible to tell sheep from goats by listening to and watching them. Sheep are sociable and peaceful animals. Goats make a lot of noise and demand to be the centre of attention. The same thing applies to people, what they say and what their actions and attitudes to others are puts them into the category to which they belong. I think it is a parable that has been made very plain to us here today. Don't you? I really don't want to upset anyone, but as I seem to be the cause of trouble I'll take myself away.'

'Very nicely done, Dorothea,' murmured Jocelin. 'Our little cousin has put you in your place, Georgina. You're a goat.'

In her room Dorrie put Luc on the floor and gave him some toys to play with. She took off the dress she was wearing, removed all items of clothing that had been given her and put them in one of the drawers of the dressing table. Shoes she put neatly side by side under it. She then dressed in the clothes she had worn on the journey to Apsley. Was that really only a couple of months ago? From the bottom of her wardrobe she took the bag into which she had packed the things she had brought from home and refilled it with the rest of her old clothes. She gave a wry smile. What other disparaging things would Georgina find to say if she could see her now?

A rap on the door, a voice saying, 'Dorothea, are you there?' It was Jocelin.

Dorrie opened the door. 'What do you want?' she said.

'I wanted to see if . . . what are you wearing?'

Dorrie gave a sardonic chuckle. 'My *own* clothes, the sort you might expect the daughter of a stable boy to wear.'

'Ah come on, you know I would never speak to you like that. Can I come in? I want to talk to you.'

Dorrie opened the door wide and stood back to let Jocelin in.

'What's this?' he said when he saw the bulging bag on her bed.

'Luc and I are going home. It was a grave mistake when I accepted your father's offer to come and live here. I cannot stay any longer. Georgina hates me too much.'

Jocelin turned the dressing table chair so that he could sit and face Dorrie. 'I do apologise for Georgina,' he said. 'She has always been difficult. Spoiled rotten as a kid, she never seems to have grown out of it and seems to think that everything runs to her agenda. Couldn't you try again to put up with her?'

'No, I'm sorry, Jocelin, it would never work. I'm going home.'

'Drastic action, how do you plan to get there?'

'I shall put Luc in the pushchair and walk.'

'But that would be about twenty miles wouldn't it? You're crazy.'

Dorrie sat on her bed. 'No, I'm not. At three miles an hour it would take me seven hours. If I start early I can be home by tea time.'

Jocelin said nothing. Then he began to smile, the smile turned into a chuckle and then a laugh. 'I've got to hand it to you, Dorothea,' he said when he could control his mirth. 'There aren't many people in the world like you and I'm so glad I've met you. Georgina is not the easiest person to live with and you've kept your temper when I wouldn't have. I can't blame you for wanting to opt out now. But I can't see you walking all that way. It's too far and it would take you much longer than you think, so I'll take you. When do you want to leave?'

'You'll take me? But what about your petrol ration?'

'That's no problem. You don't have to worry about that. So tell me, when do you want to go?'

The chance to go home by car was something Dorrie hadn't thought about. She had thought of the walk she had intended to take and though she told Jocelin she would be home by teatime knew very well that it was unlikely. It would be so much easier to accept his offer of a lift.

'I had planned to go early. I will have things to do when I get home.'

'All right, be ready and waiting at six in the morning.'

'You don't have to do this, Jocelin.'

'Oh yes I do. Will you be coming down to dinner?'

'No. Please make my excuses.'

*

Jocelin's car was not in the same league as his father's. Alasdair had a Bentley, Jocelin's was a low slung sports model, but Dorrie had no problems with that. It was taking her home and that was all she cared about. He had been waiting for her at six that morning and feeling like a thief she stole out of the back door of Apsley Hall to join him in the stable yard where he kept his car.

'What are you going to do and how are you going to keep yourself and Luc?' asked Jocelin when they were on their way.

'I'll probably get a part time job and I do have the garden.'

'But a garden isn't going to provide a wage.'

'You'd be surprised. The nation has to be fed you know. Your gardener told me that greengrocers in the town would buy my produce. I already sell to the shop in the village, but the ones in town would come and collect so I wouldn't have the problem of taking it to them.'

'But it's not . . .'

'. . . the sort of life for a young woman? Yes, that's what your father said, but it's the way I was brought up. Never buy what you can grow or make yourself. Don't worry, Luc and I will be all right.'

They drove through the village before most of its residents were awake let alone up and out of bed. Dorrie leaned forward to look at the shop as they passed by. Locked and shuttered it had not changed. When they reached the gate to the common and Leanacres, Jocelin stopped the car and turned to look at her.

'Are you sure this is where you want to go?' he said.

'Yes, we're almost there,' said Dorrie. 'I'll open the gate.'

There had been a time not so long ago when Garnet would have been waiting for her when she got to the common. Would he ever be there again?

Back in the car Jocelin drove slowly along the track.

'But it's desolate, Dorothea,' he said as he looked around. 'I see why father asked you to come and live with us.'

'It's not desolate. It's full of life,' said Dorrie. 'There are birds and rabbits and foxes and goodness only knows what else. How can it be desolate?'

When the cottage came in sight Jocelin slowed the car even more.

'Tell me you don't live *there*,' he said.

'I do, I do, and happy I am to see it. Come on Luc we're home.'

Out of the car Dorrie reached for the key hidden on a beam in the roof of the porch. Jocelin followed her and the little boy inside. There he watched as she dumped her bag on the table then set about lighting a fire.

'Sit down, Jocelin,' she said. 'I'll make some tea when the kettle boils. The only thing is that you'll have to drink it without milk. We always do.'

'How did you know there would be any tea here? You've been away for weeks.'

'I gave my friend in the village a spare key. She said she would come up from time to time to see that everything was all right so it was only civil to leave something for her.' When the kettle was hung on the hook and the flames of the fire greedily licking at it she said, 'While we wait for it to boil come with me and I'll show you around.'

A doubtful looking Jocelin trailed behind an excited Dorrie.

'As you see,' she said. 'This little valley is green, well it is in spring and summer. It's not the same as the land around it because it's fed by a couple of springs. One is sweet water that we use for drinking. These are the paddocks that my parents cleared of scrub and here is my garden. Not as big as yours, but it will provide vegetables for us throughout the year as well as some to sell.'

'But you can't live on vegetables.'

'And we don't. There are rabbits, pheasants and pigeons for meat, blackberries and whortleberries for free and raspberries and blackcurrants in the garden.' Dorrie laughed. 'And then there are eggs from the hens and a carcase if I decide to kill one.'

'I'd say that you had every intention to come home again. So why did you let father persuade you to go to Apsley?'

'I thought I owed it to Luc to give him the chance of a better start in life. I thought I'd try it, but as soon as Georgina started to pick on me I knew it was wrong and all I wanted to do was come home.'

'Well, right or wrong, Dorothea, I'm very glad I had the chance to meet you. Can I come and visit you again?'

'Oh yes, please do. Shall we see if the kettle has boiled?'

Chapter 28

Susan was sorting out carrots when the shop bell tinkled. She looked up. 'Dorrie,' she gasped. 'What are you doing here? I thought you'd left us and were living the life of Riley. What brought you home?'

'It's a long story, Susan. How are you?'

'I'm fine. Where's that boy of yours, ah there he is.' Susan beamed at Luc and held out a hand to him. 'Come with me darlin' and I'll find you an apple.' Luc chuckled happily as he followed Susan. This was a lady he could trust unlike the one in the other house.

'It's not been the same without you,' said Susan. 'Are you home to stay or just for a visit?'

'I'm home to stay. I'm going to see Rosie now because I want to get my dog back and I couldn't pass the shop without coming in. I'll come down again when the shop's shut, we'll have a good yarn and I can tell you all about it.'

'Rosie will be pleased to see you and no doubt Moss will be too.'

With Luc in his push chair Dorrie walked on through the village. Even though she had only been away for a matter of weeks she savoured it as though it had been years. It was cosy; it was sleepy and totally divorced from the life she had led for the past two months. And as for the war, other than the plane crash, the constraints of rationing and other shortages, not to mention the tears of women who knew their men would not be coming home, as far as the village was concerned it might never be happening. She knew that if it were not for the English Channel war might even now be raging on British soil. Was the channel enough to hold back Hitler's army? Or would they find a way across?

She knocked on Rosie's door. Children laughed, Rosie commanded Moss to be quiet, then squealed in surprise when she opened the door and saw Dorrie.

'Wha . . . what are you doing here? Oh never mind, let me give you a hug.' Rosie threw her arms round Dorrie. 'Come on in and tell me what brought you home.'

Moss wriggled with joy and licked the hand Dorrie stretched out to fondle her. Luc wrapped his arms round the dog's neck and closed his eyes when Moss's tongue slobbered over his face. 'Enough, enough,' said Dorrie and, Luc's hand in hers, stepped carefully around the excited dog and followed Rosie into the house.

'Oh I've missed you,' said Rosie when she and Dorrie were settled with cups of tea. 'Are you here for a visit to see that your house is all right or are you going to stay?'

'I'm here to stay,' said Dorrie.'

'But . . . what happened to the grand life?'

'Ha ha,' Dorrie gave a mirthless laugh. 'It wasn't so grand,' she said. 'I had nothing to do.'

Rosie laughed. 'You should be so lucky. Wish I had the chance to sit and twiddle my thumbs. Just wait 'til you've got a family, you'll know all about it then. There must have been something that was good. What was it?'

'I'll tell you all about it another time, Rosie. How are things with you?'

'I have my good days and my bad days and I miss Tom on every one of them. I long for him and I don't think I'm ever going to stop. Is it ever going to get any better? How do other people cope?'

'I honestly don't know, Rosie. I can only compare it to when I lost my mum, but that was different because though I knew I was never going to see her again I knew she'd had a good life and I was happy she was at rest.'

'But you've lost Garnet too and for all you know you might never see him again.'

'I know, but we never had a life together like you and Tom. I do have my memories though and so do you. I think my best one is when Garnet took me down to the mill for a picnic. I loved it there, but I've never had the chance to go again.'

'I like it down by the mill; I love the sound of the water over the mill wheel. I would take the kids there and have a picnic but there's the pond, the water, and I'd be afraid for them.'

'Well there're lots of other places we could go so when the weather's right we will take them somewhere else. It's lovely to see you and I'll come again soon, but I want to go into town this afternoon so I'd better get going.'

Standing by the war memorial waiting for the bus Dorrie remembered the day she had first set eyes on Garnet. It was the day of her mother's funeral. She had been going home with Susan Jolliffe. Garnet, with his hand on the reins of a horse, had been standing by the memorial and had stood aside to let them pass. She had looked at him and he at her and her heart had skipped a beat. There had been no chance to falter in her walk, but oh how she had wished to linger and look again into the deep dark blue of his eyes. Time after time the memory of his glance returned and she had dreamed that one day she would meet him again. Her dreams had come true and he had been there waiting for her when she was on her way home from work. But now he was gone and though she kept telling herself that he would come home, the more time passed the more she thought she might never see him again. But then she smiled and looked down at her son, at his rich dark hair and at his eyes, just as deep and dark and blue as his father's.

'Mama, 'at's the bus,' said Luc. He pointed at the vehicle that came trundling down the street.

'Yes, darling, and we're going to get on it.'

In the town Dorrie stood outside the greengrocer's shop, she looked through the windows and thought that what she grew compared very favourably with the display of fruit and vegetables she was looking at. But just looking wasn't going to get someone to buy her produce; she had to go and ask so she pushed the door open and walked in.

'Can I help you?' said an assistant.

'I'd like to see the owner,' said Dorrie.

'And who shall I say is asking?'

'Dorothea Bartlett.'

'At's a lot of carrots, mama,' said Luc. 'And what's that?' He pointed at a vegetable marrow.

'It's a marrow, darling.

'We don't have any of them.'

'Miss Bartlett? I'm Paul Winters. What can I do for you?'

Dorrie turned to see a man with a ruddy face, hair that was white and a nose red veined. He wore a brown cloth coat overall. He smiled at her. 'I've no job vacancies at the moment,' he said.

'It's not a job I've come for,' said Dorrie. 'I want to know if you would be interested in buying some of my vegetables. Some time ago my father used to sell them in the town but I don't know if he came to you.'

'Bartlett, you say. Would that be Reuben Bartlett?'

'Yes, it would,' said Dorrie. 'I'm his daughter.'

She went on to tell him what she had to offer, at the moment there was not much other than winter cabbage that was ready now and purple sprouting broccoli that would be fit to pick in another week or two. She was planning to expand the growing area she said, and widen the choice of varieties she could grow. She would appreciate any advice he could give her as to what he would prefer.

'I shall be out your way next week,' said Paul Winters. 'I'll call in and if we can do business my van will pick up your goods.'

'Thank you Mr Winters,' said Dorrie. 'I'm sure you won't be disappointed.'

'I don't think I will. I remember what your father used to bring us and if your stuff is as good as that we'll be in business.'

A warm glow filled Dorrie as she led Luc back to the bus stop and the bus back to the village. Even if the Carteret family were not kind to her at least the head gardener at Apsley Hall had given her some good advice. She would heed what he'd said.

Chapter 29

New Year 1944 slid past the village without so much as a nod or a wink. And in turn the village, its population sadly diminished, did nothing to acknowledge it. The weather seemed to despise it and turned cold. Mornings saw each blade of grass silvered with frost and every pond and puddle frozen. Rabbits huddled together underground while small birds dropped dead from their perches.

Dorrie built a good fire and stayed indoors. While Luc sat on the rag rug and played with his toys she sewed new shirts and knitted new jumpers for him. He was now three and a half years old, a sturdy boy who was growing fast. In the evenings when he was in bed and asleep Dorrie would turn up the lamp wick, fetch pencil and paper and map out plans for the garden. If she wanted Paul Winters to buy her produce she had to convince him that she was capable of producing a steady supply. She also had to add new varieties to the ones she already grew. To choose them she studied an old seed catalogue Susan Jolliffe had given her. She turned the pages endlessly while she tried to decide if it should be this or that or both. Finally, a choice made, she tamped down the fire, turned down the lamp, blew out the flame and climbed the stairs to bed.

February loosened January's hold and raised the temperature, but wept copious tears which flooded the brook, filled ditches and gullies and saturated the ground. Towards the end of the month the tears abated, drying winds blew and the sun crept out from behind the clouds.

Dorrie opened her door, lifted her head and breathed the scent of spring, the smell of fertile earth and new growth. The land was waking up. Now the weather would improve, the days grow longer, and she would be able to spend more time in her garden. In fact she would go out now.

'Come on Luc,' she said. 'Wellies and top coats, we're going out.'

Luc needed no second bidding and soon, both clad in boots, coats and woolly hats they stepped out. Taking her boy by the hand Dorrie went to look at her garden. A few winter cabbages, their tightly wrapped leaves impervious to rain, were still standing. There was not much else other than a row of parsnips - they would taste the sweeter for having been frozen - and some carrots that had been missed. The ground was still too wet to work so Dorrie turned away.

From the house, the garden and paddocks, the ground sloped gently down towards the valley bottom where the stream, now running full and fast, bordered an area of rough ground before the wood. The wood supplied most of the dead branches and kindling for Dorrie's fire. To access it Reuben had built a plank bridge across the stream. Dorrie looked at it now and wondered if it was still safe to cross. She put a foot on it and tested it with her weight. It was sound. Slowly and carefully she led Luc across. It was the first time he had been in the wood since he could walk and Dorrie was bombarded with questions. 'What's this, Mama?' when he picked up twigs that were encrusted with moss. 'What's that, Mama?' when a woodpecker drummed on a tree. He scuffed through the debris of dead leaves. He picked up small twigs to add to the sack into which Dorrie was gathering wood.

And then there were snowdrops, a scattering of delicate green and white flowers among the trees. 'The first flowers of the year,' said Dorrie. 'They're called Snowdrops, Luc. Do you remember the snow? Don't you think they look like it? We'll take one or two and put them in a jar so you can look at them and remember today.'

They went home then, across the stream up to the house and there, waiting for them on the doorstep, was Jocelin. 'You left this behind,' he said as he took a large box from the back of his car.

'I left nothing that belonged to me,' said Dorrie.

'Ah, but you did. The clothes that you were given were not on loan, they belong to you and you must have them.'

'You're very kind, but I am not a charity case.'

Jocelin smiled and shook his head. 'I would not insult you by treating you as one. I like you, Dorrie. I like the fact that you're determined to stand on your own feet. I don't know what the future holds for you but whatever it is you'll be all right. Bend a little this time and accept these to please me won't you?'

They were nice clothes and she didn't have that many. 'All right,' she said.

'That's it. Now are you going to make me some tea? I got cold waiting for you.'

Dorrie made tea, served it with milk this time and Jocelin stayed to talk. He apologised for his sister and said his father was sorry that Dorrie's stay with them had not had a better outcome. 'But I'm glad you came to Apsley,' he said. 'You were a breath of fresh air. Georgina's a handful at the best of times and father has his head stuck in the past. But life moves on, though you'd never know it at the Hall.'

'I was glad that you were there,' said Dorrie. 'I don't think I would have stayed as long as I did if you hadn't been.'

'Then we'll have to keep in touch. I've got to be in London tonight so I have to go now. I am rather busy these days, but I'd love to come and see you again, I just don't know when.'

'I'd love to see you any time.'

Jocelin had only been gone a few minutes when effervescent Rosie burst in, a broad smile on her face. '*Who* was *that*?'

'Hello, Rosie. I take it you met my cousin Jocelin on your way up.'

'Wow. Did I? I opened the gate for him. He smiled at me. Isn't he handsome? And what a car. You must be off your head to leave all that to come back here. Why did you? You haven't told me yet.'

'I know you might have envied me for what you thought I had, but I can tell you that the high life isn't all wine and roses. That's what people think, don't they? I might tell you the whole story one day,' said Dorrie. 'Where're the kids, what have you done with them and why are you here?'

'I've left 'em with me mam. I want to know if you'll come to the dance with me on Saturday. I don't want to go on my own. One of those yanks keeps bothering me and I need someone to walk home with. I want to shake him off and if you were with me I'd feel happier.'

'Not like you, Rosie. I thought you could deal with anything. I think the tea pot's still hot so sit down and tell all.'

Rosie settled herself in the Windsor chair. 'He's one of those men who think that flattery and a few gifts would make any girl happy to jump into bed with him. I've told him to forget it. I've insulted him but he's got a skin like an elephant. I don't know what else to do.'

'Well you know as well as I there are girls who for a couple of pairs of nylons and a box of candy are only too happy to oblige. That's the trouble isn't it? Because that's what makes men think we're all the same.'

'Ha,' shouted Rosie. 'Well that's not me. I mean it. I may be a grass widow but I'm not looking for anyone else.'

'I know how you feel, Rosie. And though there's no one to sleep beside me I feel the same way as you. I will come to the dance with you. Do I need to bring the gun, do you think?'

'I'm not planning on bloodshed,' Rosie laughed.

'Okay then.' Dorrie pulled the box of clothes that Jocelin had dumped on the kitchen floor towards her. As she opened it she said, 'Now you're here you can tell me what you think of what Jocelin brought me.'

Chapter 30

Dorrie was a keen gardener and had saved the seeds of many of the vegetables she grew, but now, with a list of those she hadn't and the new ones she wanted to try she caught the bus into town. The journey was not one she took very often and Luc was always thrilled when they did. The passengers were for the most part regular travellers and the driver knew them all. At each stop the people who boarded were greeted warmly and the atmosphere in the vehicle became more like that of a family outing than a group of men, women and children taking the bus to town.

Paul Winters, the greengrocer, had visited Leanacres, had looked at Dorrie's garden and had suggested what new plants she could try. When they were fit to harvest he would take all she had to spare. With this boost to her plans Dorrie envisaged a very busy year ahead. She would enlarge the growing area. Perhaps get someone to help her. All she needed now was good weather and the chance to get on with it.

The little market town was not busy and Dorrie was not in a hurry. Besides the seeds she was going to get she would buy more knitting wool. When the outside work for the day was over and done and Luc was in bed and asleep, plying the needles was a very therapeutic thing to do. Not having to add more clothes to her own wardrobe, thanks to those given to her by Lord Melchett, she had clothing coupons to spare.

With Luc's hand in hers she strolled along the pavement and looked at the displays of goods in shop windows. She had not expected to meet anyone she knew so she was surprised when someone blocked her way.

'Hello there, I'm so glad to see you,' said a familiar voice.

Dorrie had been looking at and wondering if she should buy some new shoes. Her attention distracted from a possible purchase, she looked up at the tall figure in an American service man's uniform.

'I've missed you,' said John. 'And I've been looking for you. Where have you been hiding?'

'I haven't been hiding, I've been away,' said Dorrie.

'And now you're home, so will you be at the dance again?'

'Maybe.'

'Who's this little fella?'

'This is Lucas James, my son.'

John crouched down to Luc's level. 'Hi Luc,' he said. He held out his hand, took Luc's and shook it. 'Nice to meet you.'

Suddenly shy Luc wrapped his arms round his mother's legs and buried his face in her skirt. 'He doesn't meet many people,' she said. 'He's not old enough to go to school yet.'

'Well it's so good to see you,' said John. He stood and looked at Dorrie. 'Are you in a hurry, could we go and have a cup of tea somewhere?'

'Well . . . well . . . ,' said Dorrie.

'That must be a yes,' said John.

'As long as I don't miss the bus,' said Dorrie.

They sat at a table for two in the little high street café, Luc on Dorrie's knee. John poured tea. 'When am I going to see you somewhere where it can be just you and me?' he said. 'I'd like to know you better.'

'I don't think that would be right,' said Dorrie.

'And how can it be wrong? I'm not asking for a relationship. I'd just like to get to know you and have something to remember when I go home again.'

'I'll think about it,' said Dorrie. But not for very long she thought, though she wasn't going to tell him that now.

She found John Houseman easy to talk to and would have loved to be able to stay longer, but when the tea and cakes were gone she said it was time to get the bus and that she had to go. She said goodbye to John and she and Luc joined the other passengers who waited for it.

When they reached the village and the bus stopped by the war memorial Dorrie, carrying Luc, got off. She set him down and one hand holding the bag of goods she'd bought and Luc's hand in the other she crossed the road. Suddenly the door of Susan Jolliffe's shop flew open and Susan, standing in the doorway called to Dorrie and waved her hand to beckon her in. 'Come, quick,' she shouted.

Dorrie had really wanted to get home, but the urgency in Susan's voice told her that something dreadful must have happened. 'Whatever's wrong?' she asked as she stepped in.

'Rosie's husband is dead. The boat he was on has been sunk – torpedoed - there were no survivors, all the crew were drowned.'

'Oh, *no*. Oh, poor Rosie. How dreadful. Who told you?'

'It's all round the village. She had a telegram this morning. Thank goodness she's got her mother with her. The girl's distraught.'

'I'm not surprised. Who wouldn't be? He was everything to her. Oh God, this bloody war, I hate it,' said Dorrie.

'Um, little ears, Dorrie.' Susan nodded her head in the direction of Luc. 'Be careful what you say.'

'Yes, all right. Oh gosh, this is awful isn't it? We think we're safe here. We think the war isn't going to touch us, but it does. I must go along and see her. Could you keep an eye on Luc while I do?'

'Of course I will, you go and see that poor lass.'

Dorrie knocked on Rosie's door but didn't wait for it to be answered. She opened it and walked in. Rosie's mother met her.

'Oh my dear, I'm so glad you've come,' she said. 'I don't know what to do. Rosie won't take any notice of me, just says she going to see Tom all the time and when I tell her she can't she just shakes her head and says she will.'

'Where are the kids?'

'Next door's got them for a while.'

Dorrie hugged Rosie's mum then left her to go to her friend. Rosie, eyes swollen and red with weeping turned to look at Dorrie.

'Oh my love, come here,' said Dorrie as she enveloped her in her arms, held her close and crooned soft words of comfort. In a little while Rosie's sobs abated and she raised her head to look at her friend.

'I can't go on living without my Tom,' she said. 'I can't.'

'Shush,' said Dorrie as tears of sympathy pooled in her eyes. 'It's too soon to think of things like that. He wouldn't want you to do anything hasty and you have to think of your children. They need you.'

Side by side, Dorrie's arm round Rosie, they sat on the sofa.

'Nothing's worthwhile without him, Dorrie.'

'Yes it is. You've got the children to care for. Tell me about Tom. What would he say if he were here now,' said Dorrie.

'Ha, he'd tell me to stop blubbing and to look after the little ones.'

'And that's what you will do anyway, isn't it? It's what you've been doing all the time that he's been away.'

'But I want him to come home,' sobbed Rosie. 'And now he can't.'

143

'I know,' said Dorrie. 'Because I want Garnet to come home too, but I don't know if he's alive or dead, so we have to help one another. You're my friend. I never had one before you. Your mum was putting the kettle on when I came in. Shall I go and get a cuppa for you and me?'

'I don't . . . ,' said Rosie.

'Yes you do, to keep me company,' said Dorrie. 'I won't be long.'

Rosie's mother paced the kitchen floor. 'What do you think of her?' she said.

'She's taking it badly. Can you get the doctor to give her something to help her cope? Have you got any spirits in the house, whisky or rum or anything?'

'There's a drop of rum.'

'That'll do, put some in her tea, just a drop mind, not too much or she won't drink it.'

Tea was made and poured and a dash of rum put in the cup for Rosie.

Dorrie carried a tray with the two cups of tea, put it on a coffee table and handed one of the cups to Rosie.

'I don't really want this,' said Rosie.

'Yes you do. Make me happy and drink it. And talk to me because I'll have to go soon, I left Luc with Susan and goodness knows what he's up to.'

*

'How was she then?' asked Susan when Dorrie came back from seeing her friend.

'She's heartbroken, Susan,' said Dorrie. 'Tom was the light of her life. I'll say it again; war touches everybody, even in a backwater like this.'

'You're right, but you know what your father would say, "we've got to get on with it." Freda Plowman was in while you were gone; she was going on about the evacuees. Noisy, she said, and the women go to the pub and leave their kids outside. Like I said, it takes all sorts. And then she said the place was full of all the Americans that are here. And there's more coming she said. You can't move for 'em. And she reckons somethings up and that they're going to go back to France and drive the German's back to where they came from. I don't know where she gets it all from. She never seems to go out of the village. But then some folk are like that, aren't they? It's surprising how many times she's right though.'

'And if she's right this time maybe it will be the beginning of the end. If it is we might find out what happened to Garnet. At least Rosie knows what's happened to Tom,' said Dorrie. 'Not like Freda or me. We don't know whether Garnet's alive or dead. Does his mum still think he's going to come home? I did, but the more time that passes the more I'm inclined to think he might not. So I've made up my mind that I've got to make plans for Luc and me because if Garnet doesn't come back there won't be anyone else to do it for us.'

'You're right Dorrie. You've got the boy to think about as well as yourself. What are you going to do?'

'I've just been to see the greengrocer where father used to take stuff and he's agreed to buy all I can spare so I'm going to enlarge my growing area and turn it all into a market garden. You'll get first choice of course.'

'That's an excellent idea. But you won't give up on Garnet, will you?'

'No, but it's getting harder.'

'There's another thing,' said Susan. 'The girl I've got working here says she wants to join up so when she goes do you want your old job back?'

'That would be great. I'd love to come back. I really missed you while I was away. I had nothing to do and I was bored. I'd have to find someone to look after Luc though, he's into everything now and he'd be a nuisance in the shop. But I'd better go, I'm hungry and I'm sure Luc is.'

There'd be no more dances thought Dorrie as she walked home. But that wouldn't bother her because by the time she finished work in the evening she was too tired to want to dance. But poor Rosie, what was she going to do without Tom? He was the apple of her eye. Was all her gay spirit and enthusiasm for the mad energetic dancing she did with the American soldiers just a cover up for a sad and lonely heart? Grab a little happiness while you can, Rosie had said. Sitting at home feeling sorry for yourself and your situation isn't going to change anything. How many more widowed and heartbroken women would there be before the war was over?

'Mama, mama.' Luc tugged on his mother's skirt. 'Carry?'

'You're tired aren't you my love. It's been a long day. All right.'

Dorrie put down her shopping bag and picked up her son. She settled him on her hip, picked up her bag and walked on.

Chapter 31

Dorrie called every day to see Rosie and every day went home saddened because her friend showed no sign of accepting the fact that her husband was never going to come home again.

'I don't know what to do about it, Susan,' she said. 'Surely she ought to accept that he's gone. It's been nearly three weeks now.'

'People grieve in their own way,' said Susan Joliffe. 'Some go on as though nothing has happened and then break down months later and some never get over it at all. I think you're doing all you can as it is.'

So Dorrie went on calling and each time was met with the sad face of Mrs Price, Rosie's mother, the wan ones of her children, and the woebegone look of her friend. She went on calling until the day the door of Rosie's house was snatched away from her as she was about to knock.

'She's gone,' wailed Rosie's mum. 'She said she was going to find Tom and I couldn't stop her.'

'Gone, gone where?

'I don't know, but I think she means to drown herself.'

'No, no, no,' shouted Dorrie. 'I've got to find her. Where - ah, the mill pond.'

Dorrie began to run. A bunch of kids were playing in the street, one with a bicycle. She needed it.

'I want that,' said Dorrie as she grabbed the handlebars from the child. 'Get off, I need it.'

'Git yer own, this one's mine.'

'I know but I need it more than you. I'll pay you when I bring it back. I will bring it back.'

The bicycle was small and Dorrie hit her knees on the handlebars as she pedalled, but then she stood on them and got on better. She pedalled fast even down at hill. At the mill she turned on to the green sward and coming to a stop threw the bike on the ground, for there was Rosie at the edge of the water. Dear God, let me say the right things, prayed Dorrie.

Slowly she walked towards her friend.

'I know you're there, Dorrie, I heard you,' said Rosie. 'You needn't have come because you're not going to stop me.'

'Stop you? Why, what are you going to do?'

'I'm going to see Tom.'

Dorrie took a step or two closer. 'Why come here to see him? You can see him at home every day.'

'No Dorrie, he's in the water, look, I can see him.' Rosie held out a hand and stepped into the pond. 'He's waiting for me.'

A couple of strides and Dorrie was at Rosie's side and taking hold of her arm. 'Before you go,' she said, 'I want you to tell me what we have to do with your children. If you go they are going to be very unhappy and if you're not there to tell them they're going to know nothing about their father.'

'Oh, but . . . Mum can tell them.'

'And what does she know? You're the one who has to tell them about him, what he was like, how he made you happy, what fun he was and how he made you laugh.'

Never once did Rosie turn to look at Dorrie. She still gazed at the surface of the pond.

'You knew him best,' Dorrie went on. 'Your children haven't had him long enough so they need you to tell them. They need you to tell how you met, how he courted you, and they need you to tell them about your wedding and the wonderful white dress you wore.'

'They won't want to know that.'

'Oh, but they will and only you can tell them, and, Rosie, you don't need to come here to see Tom. You can see him every day because you only have to look at your son to see him, and isn't he there in your daughter's eyes? It took both of you to make those children so Tom is in them both and as long as you've got them he's never going to leave you.'

While the wind sighed, water tumbled through the mill race and the water wheel groaned as it turned. Rosie stood in the water at the edge of the pond. She edged forward dragging Dorrie with her until they were in water up to and past their knees. Dorrie kept her hold on Rosie's arm. Time ticked slowly by and she prayed again that she had said the right things.

'Did mum tell you to come and get me?' said Rosie.

'No. She said you'd gone out and she didn't know where. That's all.'

'So why did you come?'

'Because you are my really best friend, my only friend, and I don't want to lose you.'

From the reeds on the other side of the pond a moorhen swam into view then, paddling furiously, took off and flew away.

'You're too late; I've made up my mind,' cried Rosie as she lunged forward and threw herself into the water.

'Nooo,' screamed Dorrie.

Losing her grip on Rosie and losing her foothold on the muddy bottom of the pond Dorrie, with a mighty splash, was in the water too. Down she went into the murky depths. *What am I doing here, I can't swim.* Then she was surfacing, her head above water, she spat out a mouthful of duckweed. *Where's Rosie?* There, not an arm's length from her.

'Rosie, I'm here,' she cried. Kicking out, Dorrie reached for and made a grab for her friend, but Rosie had gone under again. Dorrie was going under too.

I've got to swim. Use your arms. That's right isn't it? Hold your breath. Push the water away from you.

Dorrie kicked out, pushed herself through the water and, thank God, there was Rosie. This time she got hold of her and this time they broke the surface of the pond together. Dorrie shook her head, getting the water out of her eyes, ears and hair and then, glory be, though only her head and shoulders were out of the water, her feet were on the bottom, not firm ground, but ground at least.

'Go away, Dorrie,' snarled Rosie. 'Let me go.'

'No, I won't. You're coming with me.'

'I'm not, I'm not.' Rosie began to struggle.

If I don't do something she'll drag me in and we'll both drown. If I let go I might lose her, but I have to chance it.

Dorrie's hand and arm came up out of the water and using all the strength she could, she slapped Rosie right and left across her face. Angry now that Rosie still wanted to do away with herself she shouted, 'You're coming home with me and there'll be no arguments about it.' Both hands tightly holding on to Rosie she glared at her. There was pond weed in their hair and duckweed had spread green freckles across both their faces. 'Try to fight me and I'll hit you harder,' she said.

Thwarted in her attempt to drown herself Rosie returned the angry look that Dorrie was giving her. Then when the ridiculous situation they were both in dawned on her, her face began to soften. Her mouth twitched as if it wanted to smile. A chuckle came first, then a giggle.

'You look like a clown, Dorrie. Your hair's in rat's tails,' she cleared her throat then swallowed, 'and you've got pond weed all over you.' She sniffed. 'You . . . ought not to . . . go swimming . . . in the pond.' The giggle turned to laughter, became hysterical and uncontrollable and despite Dorrie's attempt to soothe her friend, Rosie's cry erupted into a wail of utter despair, a torrent of tears and a pouring out of held back grief. Rosie lifted her face to the sky then bent her head as she sobbed – 'He's gone, Dorrie, – he's not ever going to come home – what am I going to do?'

'You're going home, you're going to look at your children and thank Tom for giving them to you and you will see him in them every day.'

Rosie lifted her head and looked at her friend and Dorrie saw that though tears ran unheeded down her face, the faraway look in her eyes had gone.

'I'm a fool aren't I, Dorrie,' said Rosie. 'I think I'd better go home.'

Dorrie pulled her friend into the circle of her arms. 'Thank goodness for that,' she said as tears of relief coursed down her face. 'This water's awful cold and you might have given me time to take my shoes off. I'm going to squelch all the way home, you too.'

But squelching was not for them that day. Rosie's mother had begged a neighbour to look after Luc as well as her grandchildren and had then - hoping that she would find her daughter there - bribed another with a car to take her to the mill. Doris had come equipped with blankets and dry clothes.

At Rosie's house Dorrie collected Luc from the neighbour, said goodbye to Rosie and her mother and started for home. She was waylaid by Susan who wanted to know what was going on.

'Rosie and I went for a swim,' said Dorrie. 'I'll tell you all about it tomorrow.' She would say no more.

*

At the beginning of March Dorrie put a notice in Susan's shop window asking for someone to help her with her garden. They did not flock to ask for the job but one man, newly retired and finding time hanging heavy on his hands, did.

'I need some new ground turned over,' said Dorrie. 'It will be hard work.'

'I was never afraid of that,' said the man.

'Then if you come up to my place this evening, Mr?'

'Me name's Jack Randall, missus.'

'All right, Jack. You know where I live, don't you?' He nodded. 'Then we can talk about it and I can show you what I want done. If you think you would like the job we can discuss terms.'

'I'll see you later,' said the man.

They met, discussed and agreed and with a shake of the hand the deal was done. Jack came; Jack worked hard, Jack dug and broke up the soil and Dorrie, watching him, decided that he was a treasure and was delighted.

Jack also bartered a load of manure from a neighbouring farmer to spread on Dorrie's garden. 'This soil needs feeding,' he said. 'But I think you already know that.'

'I do,' said Dorrie. 'My father taught me.'

Not only did Jack dig the garden, he also checked the wire netting that Reuben had fastened around the fence in an attempt to keep rabbits and the hens out. It was for the most part successful against the rabbits but not the chickens. They delighted in flying up and over to where there was friable soil to scratch in and search for worms and bugs.

Dorrie's hens ranged free and spent their nights perched high on the rafters in the barn. Because of this Dorrie was spared the expense of a hen house which, if she had one to save her hens from a marauding fox, she would have to make sure was locked every night. If the fox took just one for his supper it would not be so bad she thought, he might be forgiven, but he was never content with one and blood lust made him kill all. So Dorrie was glad that her hens roosted so high. No fox was going to get them there.

'We ought to clip their wings,' said Jack.

'If we can catch them,' laughed Dorrie. 'Ah, but then they wouldn't be able to fly up and roost and the fox would eat them.'

So the chickens still had all their wing feathers and still they fluttered up to the top of a fence post then over and down on to the garden. To protect drills of newly sown seeds Dorrie laid twiggy branches she had cut from the trees in the woods over them.

Though Jack Randall would only take a pittance moneywise Dorrie knew that getting the garden up and running and paying her back would take all her savings. But she liked Jack and as the weeks rolled by, as April gave way to May and the garden grew and flourished, so did their relationship. When they took a break from work and Dorrie made tea Jack lit his pipe. They sat side by side on Reuben's bench and Jack told Dorrie about life in the village when he was a boy.

'But now,' he said, 'everything's been turned on its head. I didn't think we would have another war, not after the last one. I served in that, lucky to come out alive. God only knows how long this one's going to go on. But something's going to happen and very soon I reckon.'

'What makes you say that?'

'There's soldiers everywhere. Can't move for 'em. They're gathering for something and I bet they're going to make a move on France. We're all in it together now. There's Canadians and Poles and Norwegians and I don't know who else fighting with us. So when we do make the push I reckon we'll send them blasted Germans right back to Germany.' Jack puffed on his pipe and sent little clouds of smoke into the air. Then he knocked the dottle out, stuffed his pipe back into his pocket and said, 'Well, we can't sit here all day, can we?'

'And if the troops go back to fight in France, will that mean that the war will soon be over? Or is that too much to hope for?'

'It'll be a long hard battle, girl. It won't be over in five minutes. Thanks for the tea.'

*

June did not bring the wall to wall sunshine that was expected of it. The weather was unpredictable. People shook their heads but did not wonder at it. Being an island cast off from France, Britain was situated between the storms of the Atlantic and the heat of Europe. What else could the weather be but confused?

There were no holidays, no days off for Dorrie in the month of June. The earth was warm and any showers that fell encouraged her garden to grow. The humid atmosphere also encouraged weeds, weeds that were robust and seemingly able to endure drought or deluge, heat or cold, weeds that seemed to spring up overnight and had to be dealt with before they took over. So Dorrie stayed at home and tended her garden. The easy time would come after harvest when growth subsided and the earth retired to rest.

Today when she and Luc had had their dinner Dorrie took him with her out to the barn. The longer branches of wood she had collected for her fire she had propped up against the side of the barn so that they could dry out. The smaller stuff she had thrown on the floor. Now she was going to break that up into smaller pieces and store it in boxes. It was the kindling she would use to light her fire.

The open end of the barn faced the sun. Luc had brought some toys with him, wooden farm animals that he played with in the saw dust under the saw horse, the piece of equipment that Dorrie rested the bigger branches on as she sawed them up. She wasn't going to saw logs today. She had been working steadily and had filled several boxes when Luc said, 'Someone's coming, Mama.'

Dorrie looked around. 'No I don't think so, Luc. I can't see anyone.'

'I hear knock, knock.' Luke hit his knuckles on the saw horse.

'I didn't hear . . .'

'Hellooo.'

Dorrie spun round. 'John.'

'That's me. I've found you.'

'What are you doing here?'

'I wanted to see you. I may not have another chance.'

'What do you mean?'

'Is there somewhere I can sit? I need to talk to you.'

'You have the saw horse,' said Dorrie. 'I'll have the oil drum. How did you find me and why are you here?'

John smiled at Luc, put out a hand and ruffled his hair. 'Hello, Luc.' Then he sat on the saw horse, legs stretched out in front of him.

'I wouldn't be telling this to anyone else,' he said. 'And I shouldn't be telling you, but I know you're not going to spread it round the village, though I'm sure they've already guessed. We're going to be crossing the channel very soon. I've no idea what we're going to run into on the other side. So while I had the chance I wanted to come and see you. You're such a lovely person. You made me feel good. I really wanted to get to know you better and now I won't have the chance.'

'Oh come,' said Dorrie. 'You were good for me too.'

'I was never with a lot of people before I joined the army,' said John. 'I found it hard to mix with others, but then I found you. I wish I could have spent more time with you. But at least I'm glad for what I had. Why did you never come to the dance again?'

'I couldn't. Rosie's husband was drowned when the boat he was on was torpedoed. It was awful, she wanted to drown herself. I don't suppose you knew.'

'No, but that explains why you weren't there. I wondered.'

'Rosie is so young to be made a widow, one more among many who are grieving for their men.' Dorrie sighed. 'Sounds casual doesn't it, but that's what war does to us. When I'm working in the shop I see trucks driving past loaded up with young men who are going off to war. I hear their voices as they sing and laugh. I wonder how many of them will come home again and I wonder how many mothers, wives and girl-friends will weep into their pillows for the ones that don't. It makes me feel very sad.'

'There will always be wars, Dorrie; it's the way of men. But don't let's talk about that. I want to go away with a happy picture of you in my mind. Tell me about this place where you live.'

While Luc pushed his toy horse and cart through the sawdust Dorrie told John how her mother and father had worked on Leanacres, how they'd eked out a meagre living. How she had inherited it after her parents had died and how she intended to make the garden provide a living for her and Luc.

'And what will you do when your husband comes home?'

'I don't know, John. That's a question I can only answer when it happens. For now, for me, for you, for everyone, it's one day at a time.'

John stood up. 'I shall have to go, but I'm glad I came to see you. If I'd had more time I could easily have fallen in love with you even though I am no more free than you are.'

'Oh John, you don't know what you're saying,' said Dorrie as she went to him and placed her hands in his. 'I was glad of your company too and I would have liked to have known you better. But it wasn't meant to be. I sincerely hope you will be able to go home when all this is over. And I too will hold you in my memories. God bless.'

John Houseman did not take Dorrie in his arms or give her a hug; he just put a kiss on her forehead, then with one last look into her eyes dropped her hands and walked away.

Dorrie watched him go then put up a hand to wipe away a tear.

Chapter 32

'Did you hear all those planes last night,' said Susan. 'I thought the Germans had finally got here and our last hour had come. And then there was all that traffic on the road. Did you hear that?'

'I did actually,' said Dorrie. 'Luc was having a bad dream and I had to get up. I heard the planes, couldn't not hear them, and the wind must have been in the right direction because I could hear the roar of the traffic too.'

'And look at it now, dead as a doornail.' Susan pointed at the deserted village street. 'I wonder what was going on.'

'I think Freda Plowman was right when she said our troops were going to cross the channel and attack the Germans,' said Dorrie. 'Jack Randall said the same to me the other day. He said that troops were gathering ready to take off for France. If they're right I hope everything goes well for them.'

'You never know what the army's going to do, do you?' said Susan. 'I thought they might be on manoeuvres, but when I got up and looked out of the window I saw one lorry after another loaded up with men going up the road. It was a hell of a long convoy. Something's up. I suppose it might be on the news later, well, if they want us to know that is. What have you done with Luc?'

'Rosie said she'd have him while I was working here. I'm paying her with vegetables. Whoever would have thought they could be used in place of money?'

'But why are you leaving him with Rosie?'

'Because he was getting to be a bit of a nuisance and this wasn't the place for him. It'll help Rosie to feel needed. I can concentrate on what I'm doing now and not have to worry what he's up to. Oh, here's Garnet's mum.'

The shop bell tinkled when Freda Plowman opened the door and again when she slammed it shut. With no pause for breath Freda gabbled, 'They're off to France now, all them lorries and the men what was going down the road last night. You heard them, didn't you? They're going back to France and they'll drive the German's out and they'll find my Garnet and bring him home.'

Susan and Dorrie exchanged glances. Had Freda wanted her son to come home so badly that nothing would shake her belief that he would? There's faith and blind faith Susan had said, and no one had wanted to change Freda's mind or say that Garnet had been gone so long there was very little likelihood of him ever coming home. And Freda had gone on believing in Garnet's return. Thought to be dead there was no evidence to prove otherwise.

'We don't know where they're going Freda,' said Susan. 'You never know what the army's up to. You shouldn't get your hopes up or you'll be disappointed.'

'Huh, I know you think I'm a silly old woman and you mean well, Susan Jolliffe, but I've known right from the start that Garnet wasn't dead. He will come home, you just wait and see. And when he does it will be a day to rejoice. I've come for my cheese ration.'

'You had it two days ago.'

'No I didn't.'

'Yes, you did. If you can't find it now you'll have to blame the dog, you know what he's like.'

'Damned dog.' Freda tut-tutted. ''Tisn't as though I don't feed him.'

'Well you would have a lurcher wouldn't you? With those great long legs of his he only has to lift his head to see what's on the table and he's a sight faster than you.'

Freda beamed. 'But he's good at catching rabbits. Any time you want a rabbit, Susan, just let me know. The ones that dog catches aren't full of shot gun pellets. Oh well, if there's no cheese that means potato pie again.'

Side by side behind the shop counter Susan and Dorrie watched Freda as she left the shop and set off for home again.

Susan laughed. 'That could be your mother in law, Dorrie.'

'And why not? At least life would never be dull.'

'No it wouldn't and she's a good sort for all that. I'll go and get my radio; we might as well listen in case the government thinks there's anything we ought to know. Maybe they'll tell us where those troops were going. We can keep half an ear on it while we're working. We might get some news.'

News they did get and before too long. John Snagge's cultured voice told them that the D-Day landings had begun and that the allied forces had landed on the beaches of France and were fighting the Germans.

'Freda was right then,' said Susan. 'I wonder where *my* boy is; wonder if he's in that lot. Oh, I do hope he's all right.'

Dorrie was silent. After a while she said, 'I hate this war. Why do countries have to go to war? I know that Hitler had to be stopped, but why did he have to start it all in the first place? Why couldn't he be happy with what he'd got? He wasn't content with killing the Jews, was he? He set on the gypsies and then thought he could ride rough shod over Europe. So many lives destroyed, and not just our men who had to go and fight, but those of the wives and sweethearts that have been left behind.'

Susan licked the end of the stub of pencil in her hand then wrote another item on her list for the wholesaler. 'It's been like this since the beginning of time, Dorrie,' she said. 'Nothing's going to change it. Power makes men greedy and they either fight for what someone else has got or to keep what they have. We just have to get on with it.'

'That's what my dad always used to say. "We just have to get on with it, maid," I can almost hear him now.'

'Told you didn't I – I told you.' Freda Plowman was back. 'I heard it on the radio. I knew all the time where they troops was going. Things is lookin' better. The war will soon be over.'

'Aw come on, Freda,' said Susan.

But there was no stopping Freda Plowman. 'Our lot are going across the channel and landing on the beaches of France,' she said. 'They'll be chasing the Gerry's back to Germany and it'll soon be over now. I told you, didn't I?'

'Yes, all right, we heard that too. But Freda, it won't be over in five minutes. It will be a long time before it's all done. Have you found your cheese?'

'No, I haven't. I wondered if you might have a couple of eggs to spare.'

'I brought some in this morning, Mrs Plowman,' said Dorrie. 'Just two you want, is that right?'

'Well, I'll have a half dozen if I can.'

*

Susan and Dorrie were kept busy throughout the day. The shop was in the centre of the village and as well as being the place to buy groceries it was where the women who came with their baskets and ration books exchanged news and spread gossip, women who spoke of secrets and rumour.

'My husband says the camp where the yanks were is empty,' said one.

'And that one over the other side of town is too,' said another.

'Well we know where they've gone now, don't we? We shall have to listen to the news to hear how they're getting on.'

'Bet they'll have a hard job to roust old Gerry out of France.'

'I hope my Jack ain't with that lot. I can't sleep at night for worrying.'

'It'll soon be over now. We shall have a good old time when it is.'

So the women gossiped and guessed and did nothing but clutter up the shop until Susan pushed them all out. 'I've got work to do,' she said, 'even if you haven't.'

It was a long day, a worrying day, and Dorrie was glad when Susan said, 'I've had enough and I expect you have, too. I'm going to shut the door and turn the sign to Closed. Go and fetch your boy and go home. I'll see you tomorrow.'

Chapter 33

Expecting to hear bird song when he woke, Garnet lifted his head. It was not the trilling of birds, but the crump of mortar shells and bombs, the sound of a heavy bombardment. Had the allies come back? Was the battle returning to France?

The bedroom door burst open and Laurent looked in. 'Pierre, get up, get up,' he said. 'The Allies are back and we must leave the house. They're attacking and dropping men behind the German lines and we are in danger. Come quickly.'

Garnet slid out of bed and into his clothes. In the kitchen he snatched up some food and provisions that Laurent had parcelled up and followed him out of the house. 'Where are we to go?' he asked.

'We will go to the woods. If we have to stay there I know a place we can shelter. I hope we shall not need it. Leaving the house is a small price to pay if we are to be free. Let us hope that is what will be. Come, we must hurry.'

Soon they were in a forest and Laurent's pace slowed.

'What about Claude and Alphonse and all your stuff?' asked Garnet.

'Do not worry about that. You should know by now that we are masters at hiding from the Hun. We will meet up tonight.'

The forest was mainly of pine trees, the thick canopy a partial protection from rain, the pine needles a carpet underfoot.

'We must light a fire,' said Laurent. 'And make it look as though we work here.'

Laurent was not a talkative man and Garnet was thrown back on his thoughts for company. Did the arrival of the allies mean that the war had taken a turn for the better for them? Were they going to push the Germans back to their homeland? And would he be able to go home? And what if he could, what if he did, would they accept him now that he was ugly? His mother would weep to see what had happened to him. What about Dorrie? He couldn't ask her to marry him now, couldn't expect her to take him back. He was no longer the man she knew, the man she said she loved. He was disfigured, made ugly by the scars left by the burns he'd suffered. She deserved better. He should write and tell her that even though he was alive everything had changed and that it was all over between them.

The days he spent in the forest with Laurent, but for the frequent forays along with Alphonse and Claude during the hours of darkness, were uneventful. He never asked why they did what they did. It was enough to do as he was told. His only concern was that the help he was able to give in making life difficult, if not impossible for German troops, was an adequate contribution to the groups revenge for what had happened to Michelle. So Laurent and Garnet and sometimes Alphonse moved back and forth from the woods to the house and back again until the sound of gunfire and of battle moved on. When Laurent said it was safe to do so they went home.

Because Michelle and Laurent had nursed him back to health and accepted him the way he was, Garnet had also come to terms with his altered appearance. Whilst among his neighbours his confidence grew and later, if a stranger looked at him twice he took no notice. He was not the only one who had suffered injury because of the war. He walked further afield, went to the village to buy bread and wine and while there talked with the baker and the wine merchant.

So it was that he was there one day when a truck carrying British soldiers pulled up. Two men in uniform got out and went into the shop. People about their business slowed in their walk then lingered to look at the truck and the driver who had got out of the cab to lean against the bonnet. They smiled and spoke to him. The soldiers with the bread they had bought came out of the shop.

'You okay, mate?' said one.

'Frattin' with the French are you?' said the other.

'Well, I might be if I could understand what they're saying,' said the driver. 'It might be French but it ain't the French I learned in School.'

Garnet laughed. 'They were saying how glad they are to see you and that you're here and they wish you luck in the battle ahead.'

'Bloody hell,' said the driver. 'An interpreter. What you doin' here then mate?'

'I live here.'

'But you ain't never a Frenchie, not with that accent, South of England I would say and by the looks of it you've been in a battle 'aven't you? Where you from, how did you get here?'

'I was in the rear guard when you lot left,' said Garnet. 'I got left behind.'

'Got left behind did you? Is that it?'

'Something like that.'

The driver looked long and hard at Garnet, pressed his lips together and murmured, 'Mmm,' then got into the truck with the others and drove away.

Garnet watched them go, saw his link to England, to the village, his mother, his family and Dorrie, disappear round a bend in the road. Deep in thought he made his way back to the house he now called home. Those soldiers would go back to wherever their base was and report him. The military police would come and arrest him. He would be hauled before a commanding officer and made to give an account of himself. He was on very shaky ground. There was no way he could prove that what he was saying was the truth. They would class him as a deserter and he would be court martialled. Or would the driver of the truck forget all about him? He very much doubted that.

He and Alphonse were sitting in the garden enjoying a glass of beer when later that afternoon an army vehicle pulled up and two military policemen got out. Garnet was not surprised. He had known from the suspicious look on the driver's face that he would not forget and would be only too happy to bring the wrath of the military on a suspected deserter's head. The MP's must have made enquiries about him at the baker's shop. Who he was and where he lived. It would not have been hard to find someone who knew about the man with the scarred face.

'Here comes trouble, Alphonse,' said Garnet. 'I think I'm about to be arrested. Tell Laurent, will you?'

He went to meet the men.

'We've been told about you. You go by the name of Pierre, don't you? But that's not your name. You're a bloody deserter,' snapped one of the men. 'Where's your dog tag? What's your name and why are you here.'

'Garnet Plowman, Private. 52749654, Royal Signals.' Garnet held up the hem of his jacket. 'My dog tag's here. I'm not a deserter and it's a long story and I'm not going to tell you.'

'Don't you get cheeky with me son, I'm taking you in. You could have picked up a dog tag anywhere. It ain't yours. You're a deserter. I can tell 'em a mile off. Dirty, yellow, lily livered scum. I hate people like you. Come on.'

One either side of him the policemen marched Garnet to the army truck, opened a door and pushed him in. One got in beside him while the other got into the driver's seat.

Chapter 34

Garnet stood to attention and faced the commanding officer at the field station to which the military police had taken him.

'Name, rank and number,' barked the officer.

'Garnet Plowman, private, number 52749654, Royal Signals, sir.

'Proof of identity?'

'Here.' Garnet tugged at the hem of his jacket.

'I hardly think so.'

'If I could have a pair of scissors, sir, I can show you.'

'Scissors?'

'Or a knife.' Scissors were found, the hem of Garnet's jacket slit open and his dog tags pulled out. 'It was the only safe place to keep it, sir,' said Garnet.

'I see,' said the officer as he read the inscription. 'Why are you in France and not with your unit?'

Garnet was trying to explain in as few words as possible what had happened to him when the door to the room opened and the arrival of a sergeant temporarily stopped proceedings. He went straight to the officer and handed him a piece of paper. 'For your urgent attention, sir,' he said.

The officer threw the pen that he was turning over in his hand on to his desk. He took the paper from the sergeant, unfolded it and read what was on it. He stood up, said, 'Stand easy, private. I'll be back,' and left the room.

Garnet allowed himself to relax a little. What the heck was going on? Why don't they get on with it and charge me? I don't think they shoot deserters now, do they? Not that I am a deserter, but how am I going to prove that? I suppose it'll be prison, but if it is they'll send me back home won't they? Well that won't be so bad, at least I might get to see my mum.

He looked around the room. The military had taken over a house and some of the owner's property was still in it. There was a picture on the wall behind the officer's desk, an oil painting of a street scene on a rainy day. Colours were vibrant and in total contrast to the stark browns and khaki of army furnishings, and of the uniforms of the two men he knew were standing behind him.

The sound of boots on a wood floor preceded the opening of the door and the entrance of the officer. A guard shouted to Garnet to stand to attention. The officer sat at his desk, made a steeple of his fingers and looked at Garnet.

'Well, young man,' he said. 'It's a good thing to have friends and it's an even better thing to have *good* friends. I have just been told that you have not wasted time while you've been here in France and that the people have much to thank you for.' The officer leaned forward, one hand on his thigh, the other on the desk. 'You are not a deserter. Your friend who I can tell you is well known to us has vouched for you. You are a free man.'

'Thank you sir,' said Garnet.

That could only mean that Alphonse had wasted no time in letting Laurent know that he had been arrested and that Laurent had come to plead for him.

'When I say you're free,' went on the officer, 'I mean that you are not under any charge. I will have to send you to the field hospital here first to let them examine you. What happens next will depend on what they say.'

He turned his attention to one of the guards. 'Take him away.'

Garnet saluted the officer then followed the guard out of the room. He was led to the makeshift hospital where he was booked in and told to sit and wait until he was called. The hospital was busy. Garnet waited while medical staff in white coats passed and re-passed him. Everywhere there was the sound of hurrying feet. How long was he going to have to sit here?

At long last someone spoke his name. 'Private Plowman, come with me.' Garnet stood up and followed the orderly. But he was not led to a doctor. 'They're too busy,' he was told, so instead of a consultation he was allocated a bed then shown where he could wash and freshen up. 'Someone will be round to see you later on so take it easy now.'

Garnet lay on the bed and gazed at the ceiling. With a bit of luck he could be going home. Though it was something he had longed for now that it was a possibility he was filled with doubts. What was his mother going to say when she saw what had happened to him? She would surely freak out. And how was he going to get a job? How was anyone going to employ him with a face like his? And surely Dorrie would turn away from him in horror. But then if that was the way of it he could always come back to France and to the people who had befriended him and who accepted him the way he was.

Noise, raised voices and a scuffle of running feet told of a new intake of casualties. No one came to see him. The day faded and Garnet slept.

Voices. Whispering. I'm going to die, Gar. I don't want to die. It'll be dark, Gar. I don't like the dark. Bernie. Then another. Gar net. Gar net. You can't go without me. Wait for me, Gar. Wait. Timmins. The squish of boots in mud. Timmins was following him. Walk faster. Leave him behind. You can't take him with you. Go on, go on, hurry.

Timmins is not alone. There are others. Grey spectres. Struggling through the mud, falling, rising again and coming on, not giving up. Moaning, crying, pleading Wait. Wait for us. You can't go. Waaait.

Hurry. You've got to go faster. Run. Damn the mud. Poppies? How can they grow in mud? Fingers clawing at his back. No, no. Go away Timmins. Faster, faster. Aaagh. Rolling down the bank. Rocks. Bushes. And into a ditch.

Can't lie here. Where's Michelle? She'll know what to do. A flower. Yes, a flower for her breakfast tray. Where is she?

A chair lying on its side. A tree and Michelle hanging there. The rope tight round her pretty neck. Michelle. Mi . . .CHEEEEELLE.

'What the bloody hell's going on here?'

Catapulted out of sleep Garnet threw a punch at the figure before him. 'Go away, Timmins, you're dead.'

'It's all right mate.' Strong hands caught his. 'I'm not Timmins and you're in hospital. Calm down, you're safe.'

Garnet was sweating, his body slick. He sat up, swung his legs out of bed and sat on the side of it. He crossed his arms to wrap himself in a comforting hug but his hands slipped. He gasped ragged breaths. Hung his head, closed his eyes and wept - blubbed like a baby while tears, unchecked, ran down his face. A hand settled on his shoulder. 'That's right mate. Let it go. Let it all out. You'll feel better after.'

What does he know ?

Anguish welled up from the depths of his soul and the tears continued to flow. How much longer were the terrors going to invade his sleep and berate him? How long would it be before the ghosts of his fellow soldiers found peace and left him alone? How long would it be before he found peace, too?

Movement, people round him. The hands that touched him now were soft, the voices low and comforting. He hardly felt the needle going into his arm. He was guided back to his bed; someone laid him down, lifted his legs, tucked him in, made him comfortable and pulled the covers over him. And then the blackness rolled in, slowly but deepening until it was dense. So dense that Bernie and Timmins and the ghosts and terrors of the night could not penetrate. And Garnet slept.

Chapter 35

The summer of 1944 had been good to Dorrie. Her garden flourished, her crops were good and the greengrocer was delighted with what he purchased from her. He paid her well and promptly and Dorrie now had money in the bank. She still worked at the shop, but only on four days a week. Rosie looked after Luc while Dorrie worked. For Rosie the initial shock of losing her husband had dulled and she was beginning to pick up the threads of life again.

'I always knew there was the possibility that it might happen,' she told Dorrie. 'Of course I prayed that it wouldn't. But now when I feel lonely, when I miss Tom and can't help weeping, I think about D-day and the wives and mothers of all those men who died on the beach and I know I'm not alone. I used to love going to Weymouth, the sand and the sea, but I don't think I shall ever want to go there again.'

'You can always come up to my place and keep me company,' said Dorrie. 'I'd never had a friend before you, not even when I was at school. They used to call me the gypsy. And then it was just me and mum and dad. And then when mum got ill I had to look after her and when she died I had to learn how to live on my own and here I am. I treasure your friendship, so don't sit at home and be lonely.'

'Life is *not* a bowl of cherries, is it Dorrie?'

'And never will be. Now there's something I'd like you to help me with. Luc will be four in August. I thought about a party for him, but I've never been to one other than Christmas at the Jolliffes so I don't know how to go about it. Could you help me?'

'I love parties,' said Rosie. 'Yes, I'll help you. You don't have to push the boat out so it won't cost a fortune.' She laughed. 'Not that money's the object these days, but getting the food might be. I'll think about it and tell you what I come up with.'

Because the weather was set fair the plan for the party was a picnic. Not the sort where rugs were laid on the grass, where there were hard boiled eggs to shell and eat and wasps that came and settled on sweet things. There was to be a table of sorts, an old door balanced on trestles, upended buckets softened with cushions for seating. Contributions from guests would provide sandwiches, biscuits and fruit to eat, lemonade for the children to drink and tea for the adults. The birthday cake was a sponge, not iced but dusted with a sprinkle of sugar. To entertain the children Rosie and Dorrie had organised a treasure hunt.

On the day of the party – it was Wednesday so the shop was shut – Leanacres saw more people on its turf than Dorrie had ever seen there. There was Rosie and her two children plus some cousins. There was Susan Jolliffe, her daughter in law and two of her grandchildren. There was Freda Plowman, but Freda came late.

'We'll have the treasure hunt first, shall we?' said Dorrie.

'Yes, yes,' chorused the children.

Rosie took a piece of paper out of her pocket and read, 'Where water bubbles out of the ground, your first clue will be found.'

'So who knows where that is?' asked Dorrie.

'I do, I do. It's the spring where we get water to drink.'

The spring it was and there, pinned to a stick that had been stuck in the ground was a paper with the next clue. 'Where is the nest where the chicken lays her eggs?'

'In the barn,' said Luc.

In a corner of the barn they found a nest of eggs and in between them a rolled up paper tied with ribbon.

'Five mummy paces from the apple tree. Turn left. Four more paces then dig,' read Rosie. 'Ooh kids, we've got to dig for buried treasure. Isn't that exciting? You'll have to help me so come on.'

With a shovel that had been conveniently left where the treasure was buried, Rosie dug. The children crouched around her and watched as each shovelful of dirt was cast aside. 'I think I've found something,' said Rosie at last and working carefully she uncovered the lid of a box. She put the shovel aside and lifted the box out of the hole. Then she carried it to the grass path beside the garden and put it down.

'You're the boy with the birthday, Luc. Would you like to open it?'

Inside the box were little parcels wrapped in shiny paper. Each one contained a toy and a sweet. There was one for each child. To excited ooh's and ah's they opened them.

'Such little things please them, don't they?' said Susan. 'Won't it be nice when we can get them something better?'

It was time for tea then. Freda hadn't arrived. They waited for her but wondering what kept her gave in to the children's clamour for cake. And then there she was on the track, running a bit then walking, then running again until at last, out of breath, she was among them.

'Hold on 'til you get your breath back, Freda. Whatever were you running for?'

'I . . . had a . . . a letter . . . from Garnet,' gasped Freda.

'*What!*' Dorrie jumped up and almost sent the makeshift table and all the food flying, but quick hands grasped and held it. 'What did you say?' asked Dorrie.

A beatific smile beamed across Freda Plowman's face. She had regained control of her breath and now the words fell out at speed. 'I had a letter from Garnet. He's in a convalescent home. He's still alive. I said he was, didn't I? I told you, I told you. I never doubted it. Oh I am so happy.'

Stunned at this sudden turn of events Dorrie sat down suddenly. Her voice no more than a whisper she said, 'I don't believe it.'

'Oh, it's true,' said Freda.

'Well, where is he? Is he in England or still in France? And if he's in a convalescent home he must have been hurt.'

'He's in England.'

'And is he going to come home?'

'He didn't say. He just said that he was all right and that he'd write again.'

Susan Jolliffe watched Dorrie and Freda as they talked. It was obvious that Dorrie had lost all interest in her son's birthday tea.

'Why don't you two go indoors Dorrie? I'm sure you've got lots to talk about and Rosie and I can look after the children.'

'But I ought to . . .'

'Ought to talk to Freda. Off you go.'

'I'd gone into the town,' said Freda when she and Dorrie were sitting in Dorrie's living room. 'And when I got back the letter was on the mat. I recognised his writing, couldn't believe it at first. I had to read it two or three times before I could and then I looked at the date and then I knew he must be alive because it was only a couple of days ago that he wrote it.'

'Well whereabouts is he? Can you go to see him?' asked Dorrie.

'I don't think he wants me to. He didn't put any address, but I know he's in England because it was one of our stamps on the envelope and if he was still in France it would have been something else.'

'That's odd, and it means that you can't even write to him. You'll have to wait until he writes to you.'

'I know.' The happy look on Freda's face became puzzled. 'Do you think something awful's happened, like he's lost a leg or something?'

'I don't know, Mrs Plowman. But let's not think of that. He's alive and that's the main thing.' Dorrie looked at Garnet's mother and saw her worried frown. On an impulse she got up and wrapped her arms round her. 'You believed all along that he would come home, didn't you, and now you just have to wait until he does.'

'You're a good girl, Dorrie. I don't wonder why Garnet chose you.'

'I'm glad you think so. Now, I think we'd better go and see if there's any of the birthday cake left, don't you?'

Chapter 36

Every day since Freda Plowman had burst in upon the birthday party with the news that Garnet was still alive Dorrie hoped and prayed for more news of him. But when none came her days were tinged with sorrow. When she worked at the shop her attention often strayed from the customer she was serving while her eyes searched the village street. Was it too much to hope to see Freda, her face beaming with joy, bringing news of Garnet's return? The balmy days of August faded and September came in with tears on its face.

'Looking for him will not bring him home any quicker,' said Susan Jolliffe when she saw Dorrie's gaze stray to the street again. 'It is Garnet you're looking for, isn't it.'

'Yes it is,' said Dorrie. 'But I'm worried. They say no news is good news, but I think that in this case no news means that something's wrong.'

'What makes you think that?'

'If there was nothing wrong I would think the first thing Garnet would want would be to see his mother. Apart from telling her that he's in England he hasn't told her where. Surely he would so that she could go to him. He hasn't and she must be worried sick.'

'Men are hopeless at writing letters. I expect he'll just turn up one day and give Freda a shock. There's nothing you can do about it so forget it. Like I said, longing for him won't get him here any quicker. Go and turn the sign to Closed and come and have your lunch.'

Dorrie went to the door of the shop and turned the sign around. The bus from town had just arrived and people were getting off. Dorrie took a last long look down the street then turned away and went to join Susan. She didn't see the man carrying a holdall walk down the street, his hat pulled low and his collar turned up, didn't see the way he kept his head lowered, looked neither left nor right and acknowledged no one.

*

Freda Plowman was peeling potatoes when she heard the front door slam. 'That's not you already is it, Frank? You're too early. You'll have to wait.'

'Hello, Mum.'

Freda dropped the knife and the potato she was peeling and grabbed the edge of the table. 'Garnet,' she cried. 'What . . . why . . .' She wheeled round and grabbed him, held him tight, buried her face in his coat and wept. Great gusty sobs shook her small body.

'It's all right, Mum. I'm here at last.'

'My boy, my boy, I never doubted that you'd come home.' Freda lifted her head to look at him. Shock took her breath away. In a hoarse whisper she said, 'My God, what have they done to you?'

'It's called war, Mum. It's what happens. I wasn't the only one to be hurt.'

For a long moment Freda said nothing, then, a false smile lighting up her face she gabbled, 'I'll make a cup of tea, I'm sure you must want a cup of tea. Your father will be in soon. What would you like to eat? I haven't got much.'

'Come here, Mum. Tea can wait.' Garnet pulled his mother into his embrace. 'I never stopped thinking about you and dad. I knew you would be worried, but there was no way I could send you a letter.'

'But you never did when you were back in the home. You could have told me where it was. I could have come to see you there.'

'No. I knew that the sight of my face would upset you and it was better that you should see me first when we were at home.'

'What happened?' Freda put up a hand and gently touched his scars.

'Mum, you don't want to know. War is a horrible thing. I don't want to talk about it. In France I was looked after by some very kind people. If they hadn't done that I wouldn't be here now, but I am and though the face isn't pretty it's still me.'

'I will make that tea. I want one if you don't, so sit down.'

Freda was the proud possessor of an oil stove and the tin kettle of water she put on it was soon singing. When the tea was made she poured some for Garnet and for herself.

'You'll be going to see Dorrie, won't you?' Freda paused, looked at Garnet then added, 'and the little boy.'

'Boy, what boy?'

173

'Dorrie has a son. His name is Lucas and you're his father.'

Garnet put his cup down on the table and stared at his mother. 'I can't be. You know I can't. She must have lain down with someone else.'

'No, Garnet. Dorrie is not that sort of girl. Luc is your son.'

Garnet stared at the cooling liquid in his cup. 'How can I go to Dorrie with a face like mine? She'd be horrified. It wouldn't be fair. She should find someone else.'

'But she's longing to see you.'

'How do you know, has she said she is?'

'She doesn't have to say, it's plain to see. It's in her eyes and the things she does. You would be very silly to let her go.'

Garnet sighed. 'I'll have to. I would need a job and I don't know if I will ever be able to get one. I mean, who would employ a man like me? And a man can't look after a family without money to keep them.'

'You can make all the excuses you like, Garnet Plowman,' said his mother, 'but Dorrie Bartlett is the girl for you.'

Garnet stood and picked up his holdall. 'I take it I can have my old room; you haven't got a lodger in it, have you? And I hope you haven't got rid of all my clothes because I've only got what's in this bag.'

Knowing that any more conversation which included mention of Dorrie was out of the question, Freda followed her son's lead. 'I've kept your room as it was,' she said. 'The bed's made up and your clothes are still in the chest of drawers or hung up. Did you want anything to eat? You didn't say.'

'Not now, Mum. I had a good breakfast.'

Garnet went to his room and a short while afterwards his father came home. Freda still sat at the table. She looked up at her husband. 'The lad's home,' she said. 'Gone to his room, best we leave him.'

'Why, what's wrong?'

'I'll leave you to find out when you see him. But I'm thinking the damage is not only going to be what shows. We shall have to tread careful.'

There was no cooked dinner for Frank Plowman that day. All thought of what she should be doing had gone out of Freda's head when she saw what had happened to her son. So Frank had to make do with bread and the tail end of the cheese ration . . . again.

When he'd eaten and gone back to work Freda put on her coat and went along to the shop.

'What's happened, Freda?' said Susan when she saw Freda's long face. 'What wrong? Did you lose a shilling and only found a penny?'

'Garnet's home.'

'*What*? Shouldn't you be jumping for joy? Wait, I'll go and get Dorrie.'

'I'm here,' said Dorrie. 'What did you want, Mrs Plowman? What's the dog eaten now?'

'Garnet's home,' said Freda. 'But don't get excited. He's not the man he was and I think it will be some time before you see him.'

'He's home,' gasped Dorrie. 'Why won't I see him, what's wrong?'

'Why does everybody say "what's wrong?" Everything's wrong.' There were tears in Freda's eyes. 'He's been hurt. His face looks like it's been burned. He's been hiding from the German's and . . . and . . . I don't know what to do.' Freda sat down suddenly on the shop chair, covered her face with her hands and wept.

Susan put her arms round the woman. 'He's obviously been through a lot,' she said. 'You'll have to give him time to come to terms with it all. We don't know what our men are going through and everyone is suffering in one way or another. I'm afraid he won't be the only one. But he will recover. It will take time, it will take time.'

'I know you always believed that he wasn't dead,' said Dorrie. 'You've been proved right. Now you just have to be patient and be kind and look after him.' She hesitated before asking, 'When will I be able to see him?'

'That's just it.' A tearful Freda looked up at Dorrie. 'He doesn't want to see you, doesn't want to see anybody. I told him about you and Luc and that Lucas was his son. But he wouldn't talk about it.'

Susan saw the stricken look on Dorrie's face. 'I think you'll find that he will want to see you both. It's just that it's too soon.' She turned to Freda. 'Was there something you wanted?'

'No. I just had to tell somebody. I'll go home now.'

Without another word Freda got up, walked to the door, opened it, and unlike the way she usually banged it shut, closed it quietly behind her.

Chapter 37

Garnet Plowman lay on his bed and listened to the sounds of home, sounds that had been nothing more than a memory for so long. Outside his window sparrows chattered. Such busy little birds he thought, wonder what they're saying? Downstairs he could hear his mother moving about, could hear the clatter of china as she cleared away their tea things then the murmur of her voice as she spoke to her cat, the one that had been a kitten when he'd left to join the army. He could smell the lavender scented furniture polish she used, a faint aroma that filled the house. There was also the lingering odour of cooking and of clean washed and ironed clothes that were draped on a clothes horse to air in front of the fire.

Suddenly a door banged. It was followed by the regular beat of footsteps on the path outside. His mother had gone out. Garnet sighed and relaxed. He had nothing to do, nowhere to go, no one to see and knowing that at last he was safe, he was at home and in his own bed, gave himself up to sleep.

How long he slept he didn't know, but when he woke a glance through the window told him that it was late evening. The sky had changed from azure to a deep blue. A star, no, not a star, the planet Venus, winked at him. Except for an occasional sleepy chirrup the sparrows had ceased their chatter. From somewhere in the house he heard the hum of voices. His father was home.

Garnet pushed back the covers and sat on the edge of his bed. He stood up and went to look out of the window. The garden, what he could see of it in the light of evening, looked much the same as it always had. Fruit bushes, red and black currants and gooseberries, crouched side by side. At the far end of the vegetable plot were his father's ferret pens. And there was the apple tree, there had been a swing hanging from it when he had been a child, a swing which children sat on and laughed as they went higher and higher, a swing and children at play. He could hear echoes of their laughter. A swing and a rope . . . but not the rope that choked the life out of the kind and gentle woman who had nursed him back to health, the woman who had put on her other mantle and went out at night to set traps to snare and kill the oppressors who had taken over her land. The ghostly white form of a barn owl flew silently across Garnet's line of vision. Michelle. He turned away.

He tried on the clothes his mother had kept for him. They still fitted, if anything were a little on the loose side. He chose a pair of dark trousers and a navy blue jumper and put them on. The donkey jacket he used to wear for work was there. He would need that later. He picked it up and took it with him when he went down the stairs.

'Hello dad,' he said.

Frank Plowman got up from his chair. 'Garnet, your mother told me you were home.' Frank was not a demonstrative man, but some greeting was called for. Hesitantly he reached out then took his son into his arms. 'I'm so glad you were spared to come back to us,' he said. 'We had to wait a long time.' He loosened his grip then patted his son on his shoulder and resumed his seat.

'I think I'll go for a stroll,' said Garnet.

'But . . . but it's a bit late,' said his mother. 'We're just going to bed.'

'You don't have to wait up for me. I just want some fresh air. I seem to have done nothing but sleep since I got home. It must be because I'm back in my old room.'

Garnet slid his arms into the sleeves of his jacket. 'I'll see you tomorrow.'

*

'I'm giving you my notice, Susan,' said Dorrie. 'I want to spend more time at home.'

'*You what*? You can't leave me, Dorrie. What am I going to do?' said Susan.

'I thought about that and you could ask Rosie. I already suggested it to her. She thought it was a good idea. Her mum would look after her kids if she came to you.'

'Sounds like a done deal. You're doing my hiring and firing now are you?'

'No, Susan, I'm not. It was just a thought and you may have someone else in mind. Rosie would understand if you had.'

'Dorrie, I don't want to lose you. What's wrong?'

Opening a box Dorrie began to stack the pots of jam she took from it on to a shelf. She was agitated and worked swiftly.

'Garnet's mum said that he didn't want to see me. I can't stay here and listen to Freda talk about him when she comes in, because you know she won't be able to help herself. If I'm at home I won't see anybody and won't have to listen to gossip.'

'My dear girl, I'm so sorry. We all thought it would be such a marvellous day when he did come home, didn't we? Well, I do understand and if that's the way it is and it's going to help, I shall miss you but I'm not going to stop you. When do you want to go?'

'I'll stay until you can get someone to replace me.'

*

Jack Randall pedalled his bicycle up to Leanacres whether Dorrie asked him to or not. 'I love the place,' he said. 'It's so peaceful. You'd never know there was a war on but for the rations and not being able to get what you want sometimes.'

Dorrie agreed with him. Not working at the shop meant that there was no danger of running into Freda Plowman or of having to listen to any of her accounts of what Garnet was doing. There were also no probing questions from nosy neighbours to answer. In fact, life in the peaceful atmosphere of Leanacres was just what she needed.

On a fine October morning Dorrie and Jack were digging up the main crop potatoes. When they paused and stood for a moment's rest Dorrie said, 'I was wondering whether to turn over a bit more ground. Potatoes do well here and there's plenty of room in the barn to store them. What do you think?'

'I think that's a very good idea. It's a crop that doesn't take up too much of your time and you would be free to look after the more delicate stuff. You've got a good little business going here. Even when the men come back from the war and start to dig their own gardens again there are always those in town who either don't know how or haven't got room. When there's a need and you can fill it you're in.'

'Next time you come up we'll mark out a plot and make a start then.'

'We will.'

All the potatoes lifted sorted and stored, Jack pedalled off along the track on his way home to supper and afterwards a pint in the pub. Dorrie got a meal for her and Luc and when they had eaten made tea and carried a mug of it out into the garden. The evening sun shone on the back of the house. The stones were hot and reflected the heat. Dorrie sat on Reuben's bench.

As she sipped her tea she thought about Garnet. Freda had said there had been an accident and Garnet's face had been burned and was scarred. But that was no reason to hide away, though apparently that is what he was doing. He slept all day Freda said, and only got up to go out and walk at night. He was never going to get better like that. Sooner or later he had to face up to the fact that he would need to get a job, and even if he became a night watchman he would still have to rub shoulders with others. It was now – Dorrie counted on her fingers – at least six weeks since he had come home. Surely if he loved her at all he could have come to see her. Did he still love her, or had he found someone else in France? She had to know. If he wouldn't come and tell her she would have to go and ask him.

The next time Dorrie went to the village she went to see Freda Plowman. There was no danger of seeing Garnet, for didn't he sleep all day? Would Freda do her a favour? When she told Garnet's mother what she wanted Freda said that would be fine and arrangements were made. Dorrie went next to see Rosie to ask if she could leave Luc with her overnight. It was by no means the first time that Luc had stayed at Rosie's house. She had looked after him while his mother worked at the shop and he, being a sociable character, fitted seamlessly into her household. So plans were laid and one evening when most of the residents in the village were blowing out lamps or candles and getting ready for bed, Dorrie walked up the path to Freda Plowman's front door.

Chapter 38

Her heart beating wildly, Dorrie knocked on Freda's door. Was she wise in what she was doing or would she regret it? Freda welcomed Dorrie and as the hour was late she and her husband said goodnight, left their visitor alone and went to bed. The wick of the oil lamp standing on the table was turned low, leaving the room in semi-darkness. Dorrie looked at what she could see in the poor light. On the wall beside her an ornate poster declared that the owner was a member of the Oddfellows. From the mantel above the fireplace came the regular tick of a clock. Above it a large mirror reflected the shadowy shapes of other things. Nothing was clear and in the lack of light things appeared virtually colourless.

Dorrie was nervous. She twisted her hands together and when something was dropped with a loud thump on the floor above it made her jump. A flutter of nerves made her put her hands on her chest. The bump, bump of her heart was loud in her ears. What was she doing here? Was it the right thing to do, or should she have waited and let Garnet come to her? But hadn't she waited long enough already?

The scuffle of feet on a wooden staircase made her sit up. Would he be cross with her for coming? He came into the room, went to the table and turned up the lamp. He hadn't seen her, didn't know she was there. Dorrie could not hold back a sigh.

'Who's there?' cried Garnet.

'It's me, Dorrie.'

'What are you doing here?' he snapped.

'You wouldn't come to see me so I've come to see you.'

'You shouldn't have.'

'Give me one good reason why not.'

'I . . . ah . . . I . . .'

He was hesitant but suddenly Dorrie was not and the words tumbled out. 'There isn't one is there. I know you've been injured and that your face is scarred, your mother told me. I've been waiting for you, Garnet.

All the time since you went away and all the time since you came back. You asked me to wait and I have so why haven't you come to see me?'

'I'm not the man that you knew. You should forget about me.'

'I've no intention of doing that. I love you, Garnet. I've never stopped loving you. How could you think that what's happened would make any difference to the way I feel?'

'It would, of course it would. I am not the one you fell in love with. I'm ugly now. Look . . .' Garnet leaned forward, picked up the lamp and held it next to the puckered skin on the side of his face. 'I don't like the look of my face, but I don't have to look at it. If I came to you, you would see it every day and you shouldn't have to. You can't love me. I won't let you.'

When he put the lamp down Dorrie got up and went to stand close to him. Her face on a level with the top button of his shirt, she looked up at him.

'You can't stop me loving you, Garnet, any more than Canute could stop the waves. You have a son. His name is Lucas. He is four years old. You are his father and he needs you to teach him all the things that only fathers can. Come home to us, Garnet.'

Garnet put a hand on Dorrie's shoulder and held her at arm's length. 'You can't pin a child on me, Dorrie. I don't have a son and I couldn't raise one belonging to another man.'

She was angry and slapped him then. He stood back in shock. 'I haven't asked you to,' she snapped. 'I just want you to acknowledge your own. All the time you were away you were constantly in my mind. You'll never know how much I love you. It's hard to put into words, but Elizabeth Barrett Browning knew how, so let me tell you . . . *How do I love thee?*' Emotion threatened to overcome her, but Dorrie swallowed the lump in her throat and went on. '*Let me count the ways. I love thee to the depth and breadth and height my soul can reach* . . .' Tears filled Dorrie's eyes, 'I told you that once before, why won't you believe me?' She sobbed and could say no more.

'No Dorrie.' Garnet pushed her away. 'No. Go home. Don't waste your time on me. I'm no good for you, loving me will break your heart. I can't go out in daylight, children will be afraid of me or they'll mock me. I won't be able to get a job. I couldn't support you. Go home, Dorrie. Find someone else to love.'

He seized her by the arm and half led, half dragged her to the door, opened it and pushed her out. She resisted, turned and looked at him. 'I will *not* give up. I shall look for you coming up the track to Leanacres, to me and our son every day. One day you will be there. And if you don't come, I shall come and fetch you.'

Garnet said nothing, just closed the door and shut her out.

For a moment or two Dorrie stood there. He had turned her away. Well, yes, he could do that, but he couldn't stop her loving him. He could say that Luc was not his child, but would need no more than to see him to know that he was wrong. He could say that loving him would break her heart, it seemed as though he was hell bent on doing that already. She took a handkerchief out of her pocket and wiped away the remainder of her tears. No, I will not cry for you, Garnet Plowman. You cannot go on hiding yourself for ever and one day you will come back to me. Unaware that Garnet was standing by the window of the darkened room to watch her; she turned away and began to make her way home.

Chapter 39

'Dickie Briggs down at Arundells Farm says if you're looking for a job he can give you one,' said Frank Plowman. 'Best you go down and see him, Garnet.'

'Not sure about that, Dad.'

'Look lad, he's not going to bother none about your face, ha, well, he can't seeing that he's got a squint eye and a twitch.'

'I'll think about it then.'

It was all very well his father saying that Dickie Briggs would give him a job and wouldn't think twice about his scarred face, but was he ready for that? What about the others that worked there? He could just imagine the looks they would give him. But then he couldn't go on sponging off his parents, he *had* to get a job if only to put money in his mother's purse. She had said that he couldn't go on hiding and that one day he'd have to face, if not the world, at least his neighbours and people in the village. Perhaps that time had come. He would go and see Briggs. He'd tell his father to let him know he was coming, but not just yet.

November days were short and the nights long and Garnet's hours of sleep were returning to normal. Instead of sleeping in the day he forced himself to stay awake so that he could sleep at night. But it mattered not what time his head was on the pillow, Bernie Lewis and Barry Timmins haunted him still, Timmins and the grey ghosts of men who were the casualties of war. Michelle was there too, hanging from the tree with the rope still tight around her neck, and he'd wake screaming. At first his mother came running, but he'd told her there was nothing she could do and to go back to bed. She didn't come again, but he knew that when he cried out she would wake, weep for him and lie in the darkness 'til all was silent again.

He'd tried to venture out, had opened the door and looked down the street, nodded his head to a passer-by. One day he would walk down through the village in broad daylight, but for now he would still take his walks at dusk.

So far he'd not gone farther than the outskirts of the village and had stopped at the gate that opened on to the common grazing and the road to Leanacres. He had wanted to go through but always stopped short of opening it. This night he stood with his hand on the gate, hesitated then unlatched it, opened it and walked through.

He walked with memories, Dorrie by his side, Dorrie with her arms around his neck, Dorrie with her sweet lips on his. His arms around her too, her lithe body pressed so close to him that they were as one. How he longed for it to be that way again. She said she loved him, said she would wait for him and she had. She said she loved him still and always would. Would she if she could really see him, see the scars on his face in daylight and not in the soft light of an oil lamp?

He drew near the house. She had not drawn the curtains too well and there was light spilling out between them. Dare he go close enough to look in? Yes. He'd come this far and now he had to see her. At first he stood back in the shadows and could see nothing but the branching spikes of some plant on the window sill. He went closer until he could see around it. And there she was, sitting at the table, her hands busy with a piece of knitting. Her head, with that glorious hair, was bent as she watched the needles flashing in and out of the work. The lamplight turned her hair to gold. He remembered the softness of it running through his fingers.

Drawn and held as though by a magnet, Garnet could not tear himself away. And then as if she was aware that she was being watched, Dorrie lifted her head and looked towards him. He jumped back, took himself away from the light, hoped that she hadn't seen him and was relieved when she went back to her work. He stayed a while longer and watched her until she put her knitting away, until she turned to the fire and poured some water on the burning wood to douse the flames. She was making things safe, preparing for bed, and it was no place for him. Reluctantly he moved away.

The village street was deserted and silent; nothing moved other than a stray cat. But from the pub where men were drinking late came sounds of raucous laughter. Knowing that PC Roberts was going to be away overnight the landlord had agreed to a lock-in. With the doors bolted and barred he and his friends and trusties continued to drink, their tots and drams put on the slate. But time has to be called on lock-ins too, and as

Garnet drew level with the pub a bunch of very inebriated men spilled out on to the pavement.

'Well, well,' said one when they saw Garnet, 'if it isn't our local hero. He's so brave that he stays home with his mum and only comes out at night.'

'Shurr up,' said another.

'Na. My boy's in France. Why isn't he?'

'Shurr-up I said. Ee's been there.'

'Ugly bugger. An' now he's . . .'

The man never finished what he was about to say. With all his weight behind it Garnet's fist landed squarely on the man's nose. A second blow landed on his stomach and he keeled over spewing blood and snot, whisky, beer and pork pie.

'My God, what-ya done?' said the landlord.

'What he deserved,' said Garnet and walked away.

They watched him go. 'What's the matter with him?' asked one. 'Should call the police, can't let him go round doing that.'

'Got a chip on his shoulder,' said another. 'Does he think he's the only one that got injured?'

'It don't matter what he thinks,' said the landlord. 'Let's get matey here seen to.'

Word of Garnet's sudden burst of temper went round the village. 'Don't mess with Garnet Plowman,' was whispered from behind a hand and acknowledged with a nod. No one would look at him and heads turned away at his approach.

Having made his mark Garnet began to walk abroad during daylight hours. He spoke to no one and ignored the sideways glances that people gave in his direction. If anyone was brave and brash enough to give him the time of day the cold unsmiling stare they received in return quickly made them decide not to repeat it. So well-wishers gave up. Garnet was ignored and his life became solitary. He bided his time about going to see Dickie Briggs until that man got fed up with waiting for him and gave the job to someone else.

'How much longer are you going to . . .'

'Leave it, dad,' said Garnet. 'When I'm ready - not before.'

Not only did adults ignore Garnet, but children too. The village kids looked at him, said nothing then went on with their play. And so it went until the day Freda, skidding on a patch of mud, fell and broke her ankle.

'I'm sorry, son,' she said, 'but thank God you're here. You'll have to go and get the shopping for me.'

'What now? Okay, give me your list then and I'll go and get it.'

With a basket in his hand and the list in his pocket Garnet set out for the shop. It was a dull day and most of the village kids were indoors. Only one boy was on the street. He was playing with a football, bouncing it, picking it up on his foot, kicking it up and heading it. Garnet watched but walked on by.

'Hey mister,' said the boy. 'Can you play football?'

Garnet nodded but kept walking. The boy, who was one of the evacuees that had come to the village, still working with the ball kept up with him.

'What's the matter with you then, lost your tongue?'

'Get out of it and don't be so cheeky,' growled Garnet.

'No good being like that,' said the boy. 'I suppose you think that scar on your face makes you different to the rest of us. You ain't the only one that's disfigured you know.' He danced backwards before Garnet, bouncing the ball as he went. 'Are you going to be a miserable old sod for the rest of your life?'

Garnet snarled, showing clenched teeth.

'You don't frighten me, mate.' The boy stopped, Garnet too, and they stood facing each other. Garnet said nothing.

Grabbing the collar of his shirt and pulling it aside the boy said, 'Take a look at this.' An angry red birth mark disfigured the boy's neck and as much of his body as Garnet could see. 'It goes half way down me arm as well. Try living with that.'

Garnet looked at the birth mark then back at the boy. Still he said nothing.

'Oh all right,' said the boy, 'I know - it's covered up . . . for now. But I can't wear an overcoat all summer so I have to take it off and then everybody can see. You ain't no different, just that they can see you all year round.' The boy smiled. 'Get with it,' he said.

'You're a tough little bugger, ain't ya,' said Garnet.

'You have to be when your dad's a firefighter and he, your home and everything in it, ain't there when you get out of the shelter in the morning.'

'Is that what happened to you?'

'Yep. And now we ain't got nuffink. Gotta start again.'

'I'm sorry.'

'Not half as sorry as you are for yerself. Ferget yer face, it aint that bad.'

'You think so?'

'Yeh. What you doin' Saturday? Come down the rec and teach us how to play football. Will yer?'

Saturday mornings with a bunch of kids, if they were all like this one, how could he refuse?

'I'll think about it,' said Garnet.

'But not for long,' said the boy. 'See ya, ten o'clock Saturday. Don't ferget.'

Chapter 40

'What shall we do today, Luc? Shall we go to the woods and get some kindling?'

'Yes,' said Luc. 'I like it in the woods.'

'Put your welly boots on then while I get your coat.'

Anticipating a run Moss bounced around them both.

Dorrie treasured the days she spent with her son. He was inquisitive and bombarded her with questions on every new experience. He shared her love of books and though she had little time to read for herself she always read to him at bedtime. He often asked for the same story and corrected her if she slipped up or missed a word. She laughed and told him it was time he read to her.

'I will when you're an old lady,' he said.

'And that won't be for a long time,' she replied.

Boots on and coats buttoned Dorrie picked up a sack, rolled it up and tucked it under her arm and they were off. She no longer had to guide Luc over the plank bridge; he skipped across ahead of her and was away over the tussocks and into the wood, Moss close on his heels.

'Wait for me,' she called.

A jay scalded and a squirrel leapt onto and climbed a tree then sat on a branch above Luc's head and chittered at him.

'Look Mama, look,' said Luc as he pointed at the squirrel. 'It's pretty.'

'I see it. It's a foreigner, it came from America and it's chased away our red squirrels. I don't like it,' said Dorrie. She paused in her gathering of wood to look at the little animal. It was grey, it was an intruder, an import from America and it and its kind had stolen the territory of the native red squirrels and driven them away. 'Come and help me, Luc,' she said, 'I want to fill this sack.'

They worked together, Dorrie much and Luc a little, but all the same the sack was soon filled up.

'Where are the snowdrops?' asked Luc.

'You won't see them again until next year,' said Dorrie. 'Don't you remember that I told you they were the first flowers to bloom?'

'Yes, you did. I forgot.'

'But there will be more flowers. Later on I'll show you the wood anemones. I like them; they're very delicate. And of course there are celandines and primroses and bluebells and campions, such a lot of flowers. Time to go home now though, shall I make pancakes for tea?'

At home they put the sack of wood in the barn, emptied it out on the floor ready to be broken up and put into boxes for later.

'There is some eggs,' said Luc.

Dorrie's hens made nests and laid their eggs in the oddest places. These were in a pile of straw behind an old tea chest.

'Okay, I'll go and get something to put them in,' said his mother.

She came back with a bowl. 'Just what we need to make our pancakes with,' she said as she put the eggs in it. 'Come on, it's time to go indoors.'

Carrying the bowl she followed Luc from the barn past the garden, past Reuben's bench and the currant bushes and was about to turn the corner of the house when Luc stopped suddenly.

'Oh don't do that,' said Dorrie. 'I nearly dropped the bowl and all the eggs.'

'Someone's coming, Mama,' said Luc.

Dorrie looked up and suddenly her heart began to race. It was Garnet and he was walking towards them.

'Who is it, Mama?' asked Luc.

'It's your daddy, my darling.'

'Daddy?'

'Yes. Why don't you go and meet him and say hello.'

Dorrie put her bowl of eggs down on Reuben's bench. With Moss's body tight against her leg she stood to watch as Garnet came close. Luc watched him too. Garnet's mouth tweaked into a smile when he looked at Luc. He crouched to the little boy's level and rested his hands on his thighs.

'Hello,' he said.

Luc looked up at his mother then back at Garnet. Boy and man studied one another then Luc said, 'Hello,' and went to his father. With his head on one side he looked at the scars on Garnet's face. 'Did somebody hurt you?' he asked.

'You could say that,' said Garnet.

'Never mind, all better now.' Luc put his hand up to Garnet's face and touched it and Garnet smiled again. 'It crinkles,' said Luc. 'It crinkles.'

Out of the mouth of babes . . . Shot down thought Garnet. The boy wasn't afraid, just curious. And not only Luc, but the boy in the village, the boy with the birthmark, the boy who had risen above his disfigurement, the loss of his father and his home and got on with his life. I've been an idiot thought Garnet. All my fears of being rejected were for nothing. I wasn't the one being rejected; I was the one who rejected everyone else. What a fool I've been.

He stood, looked at Dorrie and held his arms out to her. 'Dorrie, my love,' he said.

She stepped forward, slowly, cautiously.

Suddenly she was in his arms, holding him, kissing him, tears of joy filling her eyes. He held her tight. His lips fluttered over her face then fastened with passion on her mouth. Once again they were as one. When he let her go he held her face in his hands and looked at her. 'I have been such a fool,' he said. 'I've wasted so much time. I've hidden away because I was afraid to face people. I've punched them, hit them, ignored them, and all the time I was punishing myself. Now your little boy - our boy - tells me it's all right. I love you Dorrie, I never stopped loving you or thinking of you, never stopped wanting to be here with you.'

Oblivious to Luc who tugged at her skirt, Dorrie feasted her eyes on Garnet.

'Now you *are* here,' she said, 'and nothing else matters.'

Nothing else matters. It was easy to say thought Garnet. If only it were that easy to make things right again, if only Timmins and Bernie would leave him alone, if only the grey spectres would let him sleep, if only life could go back to the way it was. It wouldn't and the only way to face it would be with Dorrie by his side

He pushed her away from him, held her at arm's length.

'I want to be with you, Dorrie, but I wouldn't be easy to live with,' he said. 'I have nightmares; things happened to me that I can never talk to you about. I shout and scream in my sleep. I get moody. I get bad tempered and I don't know why. I'm not the Garnet that you knew, I've changed.'

'The war has changed us all,' said Dorrie. 'When my mother died and I was left alone I had to grow up fast. Then Lucas was on the way and some of the women were unkind. They called me names. I had to grow a thick skin. But I'm still here and now you are too. And that's the way it should be.'

'So shall we start again then? It won't be easy but if you think you could live with me and my moods and funny ways, will you marry me, Dorrie? Will you be my wife?'

She put her arms round his neck, pulled him close and her lips brushing his whispered, 'Did you really have to ask? Yes, my darling, yes of course.'

Printed in Great Britain
by Amazon